Abandoned

Angela Dorsey

Abandoned

Published by Pony, Stabenfeldt A/S
Cover and inside illustrations: Jennifer Bell
Cover layout: Stabenfeldt A/S
Edited by Kathryn Cole
Printed in Germany 2004

ISBN 82-591-1164-0

Chapter One

Lauren knew she was being followed the moment she saw the dark blue car outside the school on Friday afternoon.

She'd seen the car the night before, while she was at Piper's house studying for a math test. Piper noticed it first. "Who's that?" she said and pointed out the window. "Do you know?"

Lauren glanced to where her best friend pointed. The car loitered across the street, half hidden in the shadows of evening, its windows dark with tinted glass. "No. Why?" asked Lauren. "It's just a car."

"It was moving really slow as if the driver was reading the house numbers. Then it stopped and no one got out. It's like someone's watching our house or maybe the house across the street."

"They're probably just lost," suggested Lauren, but her eyes drank in the details of the car: dark blue color, tinted windows that looked black in the dying light, a white racing stripe along the side. It looked new. And expensive. "Besides, you were supposed to be figuring out how to do question 5," she added. "How come you were looking out the window?"

"I was *thinking* about math," said Piper defensively,

pushing her tawny hair behind her ears. She bent over her math book.

"Yeah. Right," said Lauren sarcastically.

Piper grabbed for a couch cushion and flung it at her friend. Lauren ducked and the pillow bounced against the window. Lauren jumped up and grabbed the pillow and was about to throw it back, when she paused. Knowing someone was sitting inside the car, possibly watching them through the window, unnerved her. "Can I shut the curtains?" she asked.

"Sure," said Piper. Lauren found the cord for the drapes and pulled. Another pillow hit her in the back of the head.

"Hey! No fair!" Lauren protested. "You just wait!" She jerked the drapes the rest of the way closed and chucked the pillow back at her friend. For the rest of the evening, they didn't study very much, but they had a lot of fun. By the time her dad came to pick her up, Lauren had forgotten all about the car.

But the next morning it was parked across from her house. At first she didn't notice it. She stood on the doorstep, sleepily waiting for her golden retriever, Sweetie, to relieve herself. Only when Sweetie trotted toward the street did Lauren notice the car. With puzzled eyes on the car, she called the dog. Sweetie bounded toward her and together they hurried inside the house.

"How weird," she said to the dog when the door was shut safely behind them. "That car looks just like the one that was at Piper's house." But Sweetie wasn't paying any attention to her. She knew it was time for her breakfast and was already trotting toward the kitchen. "It's got to be a coincidence," decided Lauren, and she pushed the car from her mind as she fed Sweetie and got ready for school.

When she left the house for school, she opened the door a few inches and poked her head around the edge. The car was gone. "Goodbye, Sweetie," she called loud enough so the dog could hear her in the backyard, then stepped out of the house. She was careful to lock the door behind her. Her dad had already gone to work.

But halfway to the bus stop she stopped short, unable to believe her eyes. The car was parked just past the bus stop and on the opposite side of the street, its dark windows reflecting the scene back to her.

Lauren ran to join the other kids at the bus stop. She greeted the first-grader who always said a shy "hello" to her, pretended to talk and laugh with her friends, yelled at the boy who liked to tease the little kids, and watched the car out of the corner of her eye. Though the windows were tinted, Lauren thought she could see something through them. A shape she couldn't even recognize as being human. The hair on the back of her neck tingled in alarm.

"Do you know whose car that is?" she asked the other kids.

The answer was negative. No one had seen it before. The boy who teased the little kids strutted a few feet toward it to show he wasn't afraid, then spun around and ran back to the group when the school bus turned onto their street. He jostled the smaller kids aside and took his place at the front of the line. When Lauren took her seat on the bus, she looked to where the blue car waited, just in time to see it pull away.

How sick! They were just sitting there, watching us. Why would someone want to sit and watch a bunch of kids wait for a bus? Lauren opened her math book. The test was first period and she didn't have time to think about anything other than math. *It must be a coincidence,* she reaffirmed in her mind. *What else could explain it?*

But the car was waiting for her after school. It wasn't as close or obvious this time, but now Lauren was looking for it. She saw the sleek, blue and white exterior across the street and close to the corner when she and Piper were only halfway down the school sidewalk. She grabbed Piper's arm and pulled her friend behind the trunk of a tree growing on the school lawn. "Look," she hissed.

"What?" asked Piper. "I didn't see anything. Is it Tias? He's been following me *everywhere* lately." She rolled her eyes upward.

"No," said Lauren, shaking her head. "It's the strange car."

"What strange car?" Piper said. Then she gasped. "You mean the one outside my house last night? The one with the dark windows?"

Lauren nodded. "It was across from my house this morning. I forgot to tell you. It was at my bus stop too."

"You forgot to tell me!" Piper exclaimed. "You could have a kidnapper chasing you and you forget to tell your best friend? What else did you forget to tell me?"

Lauren waved off Piper's complaints. "It just didn't seem that important until now," she said. "I mean it was a bit weird the way they just sat there and watched us at the bus stop, but they didn't *do* anything." She peeked from behind the tree. The car was still there.

"Can you see who's inside?" Piper asked behind her.

"No, the side windows are too dark," replied Lauren.

"That's so creepy," said Piper. She took a deep breath. "Who would be following you? And why?"

"Hey, they're driving away," said Lauren.

"They probably saw us jump behind the tree," suggested Piper. "They don't want you to get suspicious because then it'll be harder for them to grab you."

Lauren swallowed nervously, then made an effort to shrug her shoulders in an unconcerned way. "Maybe. But now I know they're watching me, I'm not too worried about it. I'll just always stay where it's safe. They couldn't have done anything today anyway. I mean, what were they going to do? Grab me and throw me into their car right in front of the school where all the other kids and teachers are hanging out? That'd be stupid."

"You never know," replied Piper. "Be careful, okay?"

"I will," promised Lauren and picked up her backpack. "But I better get going or I'm going to miss my bus. See you later."

"Call me when you get home?"

"Okay," said Lauren and smiled. "Do I need to phone after I take Sweetie for her walk too?"

"No. Your dad'll be home then," said Piper seriously, then she noticed the twinkle in Lauren's eye and swung her backpack at her friend.

Lauren ducked, laughing. "And after I've eaten? They might be hiding in the fridge, waiting for me to open it."

"Hey!" said Piper. She punched Lauren in the shoulder.

"Sorry," Lauren said between bursts of laughter. "But you looked just like Ms. Myers, all worried and serious as if the world's going to end any second."

Piper glared at her for a moment, then her face relaxed. A smile slipped over her lips and she punched Lauren on the shoulder again, lighter this time. "Has anyone ever told you how irritating you are? And you better go or you'll miss your bus."

"Yeah," said Lauren and swinging her backpack over her shoulder, she ran toward the bus.

"Call me," Piper yelled behind her.

"Yes, Ms. Myers," Lauren shouted as she ran up the steps of the bus and plopped down on the seat. She waved to Piper as the bus left the schoolyard. Piper waved back and walked toward her mom pulling into the parking lot. *Call me,* she mouthed to Lauren and shook her fist.

Lauren only smiled sweetly, widened her eyes innocently and waved. She was glad Piper was too far away to see her hand tremble.

Chapter Two

Lauren heard Sweetie barking as soon as she stepped inside the house. She was impatient for her walk. Lauren dropped her backpack in the entrance hall and hurried to the back door. When she opened the door, Sweetie bounced inside, dashed up and down the hallway twice, then sat at Lauren's feet, her body quivering with excitement. Lauren knelt down and gave her a hug.

"Hey Sweetums, just let me grab some cookies. Then we can go to the park, okay?"

When Lauren came out of the kitchen a minute later, Sweetie was sitting at the front door, the leash in a tumbled heap at her paws. Lauren laughed, then pushed the rest of a cookie into her mouth. She pulled a dog treat out of her pocket and gave it to the eager dog. "There you go, girl," she murmured through a mouthful of cookie. Then she grabbed the phone and dialled Piper's number. Piper wasn't home yet. "Ms. Myers, this is the kidnapper," Lauren said in a deep voice when the answering machine clicked on. "Lauren made me call you and tell you that I'm stealing her away. Ha ha!"

Lauren clipped the leash onto Sweetie's collar and opened the door. She hadn't noticed the car at all when the bus drove her home. And the street was still clear. With a sigh of relief, Lauren stepped out onto the porch and locked the door behind her. She felt safe with her dog. Even though she was the gentlest dog Lauren had ever known, she knew Sweetie wouldn't let anyone hurt her. Lauren was safe as long as Sweetie was with her.

"Let's go, girl," she said to the retriever. Within minutes, they were at the park. Lauren unclipped Sweetie's leash and the golden dog ran around her in circles. She wanted to play! Lauren made a quick rush toward the agile dog and, when Sweetie sprinted away, she raced after her as fast as she could. When Sweetie was far ahead of her, Lauren slipped behind the trunk of a large tree. She waited until she could hear the whisper of Sweetie's paws racing back over the grass, then Lauren leaped out from behind the tree.

"Boo!" Shock slid over Sweetie's face and she jumped back. Lauren laughed in delight, then turned and ran with the yellow dog leaping at her heals. Finally, breathless and hot, Lauren fell to the ground. Sweetie flopped down beside her, grinning and panting.

"What a great day," Lauren said as she stared into the intense blue of the clear sky. "It's so hot, it's practically like summer already. Just one more week of school..." she said dreamily and rolled over to scratch under Sweetie's chin. "Hey, maybe Dad will come home early today. He leaves work early on Fridays sometimes. Maybe he'll drive us to the beach."

She jumped up and pulled a dog treat and another cookie from her pocket. "Which one do you want?" she asked Sweetie with a grin. Then she popped the cookie into her mouth. "Too late," she said in a muffled voice and held the dog treat out to Sweetie. Then she pulled the leash from her pocket and clipped it onto Sweetie's collar. "Let's go, Sweetums."

She wouldn't have even noticed the person sitting on the bench if Sweetie hadn't growled. Lauren glanced down, surprised. "What's wrong, girl?" she asked and followed the line of Sweetie's vision. Someone in a big floppy hat and a trench coat was sitting on the park bench beside the parking lot. And behind the person was the blue car!

This is the final proof, thought Lauren, fear surging into her brain. *There's no mistaking it now. There aren't any other kids here. The driver of the blue and white car is following me. Not Piper or the other kids at the bus stop. Just me!*

She pulled on Sweetie's leash. "Let's go," she commanded. But Sweetie tugged back.

"Come on, Sweetums. We've got to get home. I've got to phone Dad right away." Her voice was on the edge of panic. Lauren started to pull Sweetie toward home, but the dog continued to struggle. Finally Lauren stopped and looked down at the disobedient dog. "What's wrong, girl?" she asked softly, kneeling by the dog's side. Sweetie wasn't growling anymore, but she still seemed intrigued by Big Hat. The hair on her back stood on end as she sniffed the air.

"Is that the guy from the car? Can you tell if he wants to hurt us?" whispered Lauren, though she knew the dog couldn't answer, at least not in words. She peered at the person sitting on the bench. Big Hat's features were hidden in the shadow of his gigantic hat and the shapeless coat covered him from neck to knees.

As Lauren watched, Big Hat raised a camera from his lap and pointed it toward her. His finger twitched on the

button. Lauren's mouth dropped open and she stood, her hands slowly clenching into fists. Anger trickled into her mind, creeping over top of her fear. How dare this person follow her! How dare he take her picture! Without thinking, she took a step toward Big Hat, and then another.

"Hey!" she yelled. "Who are you?" Sweetie tugged on the leash, pulling Lauren closer. Big Hat jumped up and the camera fell from his lap and bounced across the grass. He hurried to pick it up, his movements jerky. Almost panicky.

Lauren blinked her eyes. This wasn't what she was expecting: the watcher wasn't supposed to be afraid of her. *Sweetie! He's afraid of Sweetie,* she realized. *This is my chance to find out who he is.*

"Hold still, girl," she said as she bent to release Sweetie from the leash. The dog was anxious to run toward the stranger and Lauren had trouble grabbing the clip, but finally Sweetie was free. Lauren straightened as Sweetie bounded toward Big Hat.

But Big Hat was almost to his car. Lauren ran toward Sweetie when the retriever stopped to sniff at the bench where Big Hat had been sitting. The car door slammed. Tires squealed as the vehicle sped away. Then Lauren was at Sweetie's side, breathing heavily. She hugged the dog to her and clipped the leash back onto her collar.

"Thanks, for saving me, Sweetie," she gasped. The dog licked her face and Lauren drew a deep breath. "I can't believe he was taking my picture! What a jerk! A horrible, creepy jerk. Come on, we've got to get home. I have to tell Dad about this right away."

Chapter Three

Lauren and Sweetie ran all the way home. Within seconds of coming in sight of the house, Lauren was safe inside with the door locked behind her. She dialed her dad's work number with shaking fingers.

"Is my dad still there?" she asked when her father's assistant, Emily, answered the phone.

"Oh, Lauren. I wish you hadn't asked," said Emily. Her voice was kind and grandmotherly and Lauren's alarm eased slightly. "He left, oh, maybe ten minutes ago. He thought he'd surprise you and come home early."

"Don't worry, Emily," answered Lauren, relieved. "I won't tell him you said anything."

"That's great. You have a good weekend now, you hear?"

Lauren smiled. "I will, Em. Thanks. You too, okay?"

"I will, Love. Bye now." There was a soft click and Lauren knew Emily had disconnected. She put down the receiver and almost picked it up again. She knew Emily wouldn't mind talking to her until her dad came home.

But she's probably going home early too, thought Lauren. *I don't want to keep her. I can feed Sweetie her supper. That'll keep me busy until Dad gets home.* She unclipped Sweetie's leash and hung it up, then followed the eager dog into the kitchen.

As she dumped the can of dog food into Sweetie's bowl, she heard the key in the front door deadbolt. Leaving the dog in the kitchen, she ran toward the door and reached for the lock.

Suddenly the image of Big Hat flashed into her mind. What if he'd somehow gotten a key and was coming inside? Or what if he was trying to fool her into thinking he was her dad so she would unlock the door for him.

Don't be silly, Lauren told herself, but she took a step backward. There were scuffling sounds outside the door and then the door unlocked. More sounds. Lauren was almost ready to jump forward and lock the door again when it slowly, slowly swung open. And there was her dad holding two bags of groceries.

A breath of relief, almost like a sob, exploded from Lauren. She leaped forward and flung her arms around her dad's waist.

"Whoa there, partner," he said, holding the bags up higher. "What's all this about?"

But now that he was home, Lauren didn't know how to start. She stepped back and opened her mouth, but the words stuck in her throat. Then, even worse, two big tears appeared in the corners of her eyes.

"Hey, Lauren, what's wrong?" her dad asked gently. He put the groceries on the hall table and pulled her into his arms once more. "Did something happen at school? Are you okay?"

To her horror, Lauren couldn't stop crying. She *never* did this in front of her dad anymore. Never. Not since she was eight and he told her that her mom had died.

It had been such a shock, to her and her dad. After all, the car accident hadn't seemed that bad and her mom was recovering in the hospital. Lauren remembered visiting her there, and her mom saying she was fine. Laughing even. But then the day came when she went with her dad to visit and her mom wasn't there. Her dad had gone to talk to a nurse and left Lauren in the hospital room. Lauren laid down on her mom's bed and waited and waited and waited. The next thing she knew she was waking up and her dad was saying the unbelievable. That her mom was gone. It wasn't until later that she understood her mom had died and that she would never see her again.

Broken hearted, she had cried and cried and cried. For weeks. Everything during that time was still a blur to her. She could hardly remember anything about it, except for the crying. And Sweetie, she could remember Sweetie licking tears from her cheeks. Then one day she looked up, saw the terrible pain in her dad's dry eyes, and understood he refused to cry because he didn't want her to be even sadder. And she stopped crying herself. Promised herself she would never cry again. And she hadn't. Until now.

Lauren dashed the tears from her eyes and sniffled. Her dad waited patiently for her, his arms steady around her. "It's okay, Kiddo," he whispered. "There's nothing wrong with a good cry now and then. I can wait to hear all about it." His words made her feel stronger and she pulled back.

"Just let me get a tissue first," she said, her voice hoarse, and hurried toward the downstairs bathroom. She wiped her eyes and her nose, and then looked in the mirror above the sink. The skin around her eyes and nose was red, making her hazel eyes look yellow in comparison. *At least my nose matches my hair now,* she thought and ran her fingers through the red mop on her head.

She frowned. "I can't believe you just did that," she whispered to her reflection. "Why would you cry over something so silly? You're such a pansy. Grow up."

18

"So what's up?" her dad said gently when she walked into the kitchen.

"Let me start at the beginning, okay?" asked Lauren. When her dad nodded, she pulled one of the bright blue kitchen chairs back from the table and slid onto its cool seat. Her dad sat down opposite her. Lauren started at Piper's house with the strange car, then told him of seeing the car in the morning when she let Sweetie out and then again at the bus stop. As she talked, her dad's face became paler and paler, and, when she told him about the man taking her picture, he reached out and clutched her hand. "So someone's been following me," she finally concluded. "I don't know who it is, but I'm scared."

Her dad took a deep trembling breath. "Was it a man or a woman?" he asked, his eyes locked onto Lauren's. "And what about hair color? Height? Did you get a license plate number?"

Lauren squirmed on the chair. "I couldn't see his hair. And he was about averagely tall. And I didn't even think about a license plate number. Sorry."

"But you think the person is a man?"

"I'm not even sure of that," she admitted. "Sorry, Dad. I couldn't see his face. Or her face. *It's* face, I guess."

"Don't be sorry, Honey. I'd rather you tell me exactly what you think, even if you don't know for sure. It won't help if we're looking for a man and the stranger is really a woman. You think it's a man though?"

Lauren's hand dropped to scratch Sweetie on the head. "It could have been either. I remember his hands when he held the camera up. They weren't tiny woman hands, but all women don't have little hands. I mean, Piper already teases me about my *man* hands. She's such a brat."

"What else do you remember?"

19

"When he ran toward the car, he ran pretty fast so it could have been a man. But he was kind of graceful too, so maybe it was a woman," Lauren remembered aloud. "Sorry, Dad. I don't mean you're not graceful or anything."

A small smile slipped across his face. "No worries," he said. "I know I'm clumsy. Is there anything else you re-member? Anything that seemed strange or unusual?"

A puzzled expression crossed Lauren's face and she looked down at Sweetie sitting calm beside her. "There was one weird thing," she said slowly. "I wouldn't have known it was the stalker if Sweetie hadn't growled. I thought it was just another person at the park. It was only when Sweetie acted interested that I wondered if it was the person who was following me."

"Do you think Sweetie knew him? Or her?" asked Lauren's dad.

Lauren glanced up sharply. Her dad's voice sounded different. A little breathless. "I don't see how she could. Unless someone's been sneaking around here while I'm at school, trying to make friends with her." She paused for a moment and frowned. "No, it wasn't as if Sweetie knew who it was. More like she wasn't sure. Or maybe she heard the click of the camera and just wanted to let me know about it."

Her dad leaned on the table and rubbed his eyes with both hands, then ran his fingers through his hair. "Okay, now here's what we're going to do. I'll drive you to school every day and make arrangements for you to go to Piper's house afterward until I can pick you up. We can walk Sweetie together when I get home." He dropped his hands and looked at Lauren with worried eyes. "And as soon as summer vacation starts next week, I want you to go to your Aunt April and Uncle Chris's."

Lauren groaned. "For how long?"

"Until we get this straightened out."

"But that could be all summer!" protested Lauren.

"It could be."

"But Dad, I have plans…"

"No 'buts'. This is serious and we've got to be careful. I'll find the person who's been following you. And I'll find out why."

"But Piper was going to have a big party for me on my birthday, remember?" Lauren hoped her voice didn't sound as whiny to her dad as it did to her. "Her mom already said we could have it at her house. We were inviting all our friends and they have the swimming pool and the hot tub. And we were going to eat tons of pizza. And then you were going to take us to the movies. It was going to be so much fun."

"Sorry, Kiddo, but we can't take any chances."

Lauren looked down at Sweetie, curled on the floor by her feet. "We've been planning it for ages," she said, then looked up hopefully. "Couldn't I just come home for the party? Turning thirteen is important, Dad. And you're going to miss me if I'm away for two whole months. And so will Sweetie."

Lauren's dad sighed. "I know I will. Okay, I'll see if I can get a week off work and drive out to pick you up. It'll be nice to see April, Chris, and the girls anyway. But if we haven't found the stranger by then, you'll have to go back to Misty Lake after the party."

"Thanks, Dad." Lauren smiled. "But you've got to find the stranger and fast too, okay? And the police will help. And really, I mean *fast*. Misty Lake's in the middle of nowhere. What'll I do there for the whole summer?"

"Hike. Canoe on the lake."

"And hike some more and canoe some more and, hey, I know, hike and canoe on the lake."

"Some people pay big money to go to places that are so peaceful," said her dad, raising his eyebrows.

"But for two months?" asked Lauren. "It's going to be so boring."

"I think you'll be surprised. Remember, your Aunt April and I grew up in Misty Lake and so did your mom. We always found things to do," he added.

One side of Lauren's mouth raised into a lopsided smile. "Yeah. Hike and canoe."

"You forgot swimming in the lake," he said, grinning, and reaching out, he ruffled her hair.

"Hey! It's messy enough already." Lauren ducked and then reached out with a fist. She punched him lightly in the ribs. "Don't mess with me," she warned.

"You punched me! I can't believe it! You actually punched me. Ooh, that smarts," her dad said and pressed his hand against his shoulder.

"I punched you in the ribs, not in the shoulder," said Lauren and cocked her head. "You better stop teasing or I'll punch you again."

Her dad laughed, then his face slowly became serious. "I'm going to miss you, Kiddo. It won't be the same around here without you."

The smile disappeared from Lauren's face too. She dropped her hand to her side and ran her fingers through Sweetie's hair. "Really, Dad, promise me you'll find out what's happening as fast as you can, okay?"

"I'll do my best," he said and ruffled her hair again. "Now let's get going. We'll drop by the police station and tell them our story, then we'll hit the beach."

Chapter Four

Filling out the report at the police station took longer than both Lauren and her dad thought it would, and they didn't get to the beach until late evening. As Sweetie ran around them in circles, Lauren and her dad walked toward the sunset. The pinks and apricots, blues and purples in the sky were a beautiful end to the hot day. They stopped when they reached the water.

"It's amazing the detail you remembered about the car," said Lauren's dad, looking over the waves reflecting the sky's glory.

"Well, I saw the car a lot more than the stalker," said Lauren, jumping back as a wave washed toward her.

"Yes, but they were even able to pinpoint the year it was made from your description. You've made their job a lot easier. Maybe we'll even know within a week or two."

Lauren smiled. She felt hopeful too. The police officer had sounded confident they would find the car soon, as long as the person didn't leave town.

That night, when they got home from the beach, Lauren's dad phoned his sister. Lauren's Aunt April was overjoyed when he asked if Lauren could come for the summer. She asked to talk to Lauren and then went on and on about how much fun they would all have. Her two daughters, Charity and Kjerstina, were apparently starting a new project and Aunt April was excited about getting Lauren involved. But she wouldn't tell Lauren what the project was. All she said was that it was a secret that Lauren would love.

I don't know if I can take any more intrigue, thought Lauren, but she didn't say anything. Her aunt was so cheery about her coming to visit and she didn't want squash her enthusiasm by letting her know she wasn't as thrilled about the summer as Aunt April was.

All that weekend, her dad stuck close beside her and by the time she saw Piper at school on Monday morning, Lauren felt she was going to go crazy. Except in her bedroom, she hadn't had any privacy at all. It was like her dad didn't want to let her out of his sight, even when they were at home.

Piper was still upset about the birthday party. "But half the fun is planning and talking about it together," she complained.

"We can talk on the phone," Lauren replied. "Aunt April won't mind. And when Dad drives out to Misty Lake to pick me up, you should come."

"What about when you go out next week too?" asked Piper. "I've never been to Misty Lake."

"You're not missing a whole lot, except seeing every shade of green in existence. There are tons of trees out there. But you can't come. Dad doesn't have time to drive me, so I'm flying out on one of those little airplanes. It would be awesome if you could though. Misty Lake would be a lot more fun if you were there!"

Lauren looked for the car after school while she waited for Piper's mom to pick them up. It was nowhere to be seen. That evening, after her dad came home and they ate supper, Lauren and her dad took Sweetie to the park for her run.

At first Lauren didn't see the car at the end of the parking lot, because it was hidden behind a gray van. But when the van pulled out of the lot, Lauren caught her breath.

"Dad! There it is!" Her voice was shrill as she pointed.

Without hesitating, he sprinted toward the car. Lauren watched in dismay as the car raced out of its parking slot and accelerated toward the exit. When her dad realized he wasn't going to catch it, he stopped. Lauren watched as he fished a pen out of his pocket and jotted down a few things on his hand. Then he hurried back to her.

"Did you get the license plate number?" she asked, excited.

"I got the first three numbers. We'll phone the constable as soon as we get home. Maybe you won't have to go at all. Or at least, not until I can go with you like we normally do."

"That would be awesome," replied Lauren.

But they didn't hear anything from the police or see the car for the rest of the week. Lauren guessed the driver was spooked by how close her dad had come to discovering his identity and was hiding out, waiting for them to be less vigilant. But the driver didn't know Lauren was flying to Misty Lake on Saturday morning.

On Friday night Lauren packed. She threw her clothes and toothbrush, hairbrush, and other things into the suitcase and squished them down. Then she put the books her dad bought her the day before on top of the clothes. Last of all, she lifted a small painting off her wall. She couldn't leave it behind. The painting was only twelve inches wide and eight inches tall and Lauren knew every square inch of it, every brush stroke. It showed a man and woman, her dad and mom, sitting cross-legged on the floor. A little girl with bright red hair was between them, walking from her father's arms to her mother's. Lauren's mom had painted the portrait from memory to commemorate Lauren's first steps and it was Lauren's most prized possession. The expression of joy on each face always made Lauren feel better.

She pulled her softest t-shirt from the pile of clothes and wrapped it around the painting and placed it on top of the books. Then she pulled the thumbtack from the wall and pushed it into a small pocket in the suitcase.

That night, Lauren and her dad stayed home. They rented three comedies and planned to watch them one after the other and eat tons of popcorn, but halfway through the second movie, Lauren's eyelids became heavy. She struggled to keep them open and finally decided to close them for just two minutes.

The next thing Lauren knew, she was waking up. She was in her bedroom, tucked under her covers, in the same clothes she was wearing the night before. She groaned and stretched, then heard her dad coming down the hallway, singing in his off-key voice.

"Wake up, get out of bed. Wake up, you sleepyhead. When the red, red robin comes a-bob-bob-bobbing along."

"I'm up," Lauren said and then, when he kept on singing, she yelled it and pulled the pillow over her head. "This is supposed to be the weekend!"

"Sorry, Kiddo," his voice came through the door. Lauren noticed he didn't sound very sorry. "We've got to get going if you want to stop at Mirabella's."

Lauren groaned. They had to be at the airport by nine

to catch the plane and her dad was taking her out to breakfast at Mirabella's, her favorite restaurant, before the flight. She glanced at her watch. They would have to hurry.

"I'll be ready in a couple of minutes," she called and sat up in bed.

Everything at Mirabella's was bright and colorful. Big paintings of plump red cats and fat green horses covered the walls at odd angles. The walls were all a royal blue and the ceiling was covered with painted stars. Multi-colored sashes draped across the tall windows, making the curtains look like a rainbow. Lauren always wondered if the owner of Mirabella's was a gypsy.

Lauren's dad teased her all through breakfast about the boys she was going to meet in Misty Lake. At first Lauren argued with him, saying all the boys were interested in Kjerstina and Charity, but he wouldn't stop teasing her until she laughingly suggested that he was the one looking for a girlfriend and that he wanted to get rid of his daughter for the summer so she wouldn't get in the way. "Sorry Dad," she said, when she saw the teasing twinkle in his eyes fade away. "I was just joking."

"You know I really don't want you to go, don't you Lauren?" he asked, his voice hopeful. Almost pleading.

"Yeah, I know." And she did know. She had no doubt. Her dad loved her more than anything. He'd always been devoted to her, just like she was to him. Ever since her mom had died, it was just the two of them against the world. And Sweetie. "It's just that I'm going to miss you. It'll be weird being there without you. I've never been there before, all alone. It's going to be so boring."

"You're not going to be alone. Charity and Kjerstina can't wait until you get there. And you know how your

27

aunt is. And besides, I think you'll be surprised at how un-boring it is."

"What do you mean?"

"Remember Aunt April told you Charity and Kjerstina had a project? Well, she's been working her heart out, setting everything up so you can do it too."

"Really? What is it? Tell me."

"I can't. It's a secret."

"Secrets! I hate secrets! Especially when *everyone* knows but me. Really, Dad, I'll know soon anyway, so why don't you just tell me? I promise I won't let anyone know you told."

"That's no fun."

"But its like torture to not tell me," said Lauren. She wiggled in her seat to accentuate how uncomfortable she was with not knowing the secret.

"I like tormenting you," replied her dad with a grin.

"I'll get even you know. Just you wait and see. I'll think of a good way to get even. It's a promise!"

"Oh, oh. Now I'm scared," said her dad with an expression of exaggerated terror.

"Grrr! It's so frustrating. Can't you just give me a hint? Just a little one. I won't tell Aunt April. I swear," pleaded Lauren.

Her dad looked at her with narrow eyes. "Hmmm. A hint. Well, let me see." He took a slow sip of his coffee. "Okay your hint is…" Then he looked down at his watch. "Oops, no time. We'd better get going or your plane will be taking off without you."

"Dad!" He wouldn't give her a single hint all the way to the airport. Together they checked her bags and got her boarding pass from the airline counter. As they walked toward Gate B21 where the airplane waited, Lauren fell silent. When the boarding announcement for Lauren's flight came over the loudspeaker, she sighed. Her dad reached over and tousled her hair as if she were five years old again. "It'll be okay," he said. "I'll call you tonight."

"Okay. See you later, Dad."

"I'm going to miss you, Kiddo," he said and pulled her into a hug. "I love you."

"I love you too, Dad," replied Lauren and squeezed hard one more time before pulling away. Slowly she walked to the gate and showed her boarding pass to the airline attendant.

"Lauren!" his voice came from behind her and she turned around, hoping he'd changed his mind. Hoping she'd be allowed to stay. "Think soldier!"

It took her a moment to realize this was her hint for guessing the surprise. She smiled and waved one more time, then walked through the gate. A few minutes later she was in her seat on the airplane. Still deep in thought, Lauren leaned back in her chair and closed her eyes. But she wasn't thinking about the hint he gave her.

Now that she didn't have to convince her dad she wasn't worried, now that she didn't have to make flippant conversation, she was thinking about the stranger.

Who is he? What does he want with me? And why? She had so many questions. But no answers. No answers at all.

Chapter Five

The airplane landed at the Misty Lake Airport, taxied to the terminal, and parked beside it. The stewardess asked the passengers to remain seated as the stairs were prepared for them to disembark from the airplane, and when they were allowed to go, Lauren filed slowly down the aisle with the others. At the doorway to the airplane, she paused. She could see Kjerstina, her fifteen-year-old cousin, waving at her through the big window of the terminal. Lauren waved back as cheerfully as she could. She didn't want anyone to know how much she wished she were home.

"Hey, Lauren!" called Kjerstina when Lauren stepped inside the terminal. Kjerstina hurried toward her cousin, her shoulder length brown hair swinging around her head. "We've been waiting forever for you. Your plane was so late." She threw her arms around Lauren's thin frame.

"My, you've grown tall, Lauren," exclaimed Aunt April, coming up behind Kjerstina. "It's wonderful to see you." When Kjerstina released Lauren, Aunt April pulled her into another hug. Lauren closed her eyes. She loved Aunt April's hugs. Her arms were strong and soft at the same time.

"How's my baby brother doing?" asked Aunt April after letting her go.

"Dad's fine," said Lauren, smiling. It seemed weird that her big tall dad was anyone's baby brother. "He's going to come out right before my birthday."

"Awesome!" said Kjerstina. "Uncle Alan is so much fun. I can't wait to see him."

"Well, let's grab your bags and get going," suggested Aunt April. "Charity's probably given up on us by now."

"We have a surprise for you at home," said Kjerstina. "You're going to love it."

On the way to Aunt April's house, Lauren tried to listen to Kjerstina talk about the wonderful summer they had planned, but when Kjerstina started listing all the possible activities in alphabetical order, her mind turned back to her dad.

What's he doing now? she wondered. *Is he sitting at the table and reading his newspaper? Did he take Sweetie for her walk? It's past time for her to go. Or maybe he's at the police station, talking to the police about the stalker again. I wonder if he misses me already? I wonder if he wishes I were there right now?*

Suddenly, Lauren noticed Kjerstina had stopped talking and Aunt April had a worried expression on her face. *It's because I look sad*, Lauren realized. She forced herself to smile. "What's the surprise, Kjerstina?" she asked.

"Oh, I can't tell you," Kjerstina said, smiling again. "You have to wait and see. But you'll like it, I promise." She paused, then unable to keep quiet, she blurted out, "It's so cool! You're going to love it."

"Give me a hint," begged Lauren. "Dad gave me one. Soldier."

31

"Soldier?" asked Kjerstina. "Oh, I get it." She laughed. "You'll never guess it from his hint. It's way too hard. How about this one: it's big and gold and…"

"Stina! That's enough," laughed Aunt April. "No hints. Lauren will just have to wait until we get home."

"Can I try to guess?"

Kjerstina laughed. "You'll never guess," she said. "It's way too cool for ordinary guesses."

"Stina, I said no more hints," said Aunt April. Her voice still sounded somewhat amused, but Lauren could tell she was losing patience.

"I guess you'll just have to wait," said Kjerstina, flashing Lauren an apologetic look.

"But not for too long," said Aunt April. "Here we are. Stina, you and Charity can help Lauren unpack first, okay?"

"Sure, Mom," said Kjerstina, opening her car door. She waited for Aunt April to open the trunk, then grabbed Lauren's suitcase. Together they walked to the house.

"Charity!" Kjerstina yelled when they opened the front door.

"Yeah," came a muffled voice from somewhere inside the house.

"We're back and Lauren's here," yelled Kjerstina.

"I'm in the tub. I'll be right out," came the reply.

"You get to share a room with me all summer," said Kjerstina to Lauren as they started to climb the stairs. "And I've been dying to show you what I've done to my room."

Lauren followed Kjerstina up the stairs and into the small bedroom. Kjerstina had painted the room since last time Lauren had visited. One wall gleamed a dark forest green and the other three were a watery red with white stripes zigzagging across them. It didn't seem like it should match at all, but with the forest green bookshelf against one red wall and the bunk bed painted red, everything seemed to belong in the room. The door was white and a red rug sprawled across the wooden floor.

"Do you like it?" asked Kjerstina hopefully. "Dad says it looks like a Christmas tree exploded."

"I love it," said Lauren. "It's wild." Paintings of brightly-colored tree branches and flowers hung in a long line across the far red wall. "Did you do the paintings too?" asked Lauren. "They're great."

"Yeah, I did and thanks," said Kjerstina with a grin. "I've been trying to learn about interior decorating and I saved up my babysitting money to do all this. Mom gave me some ideas and Dad and Charity helped with the painting. Charity wants to decorate her room too, but she hasn't decided what to do yet. Maybe you'll have some ideas she'll like," suggested Kjerstina. "She's sick of having baby pink walls."

"I know how she feels," said Lauren. "My room at home is plain white. Maybe I should pick out some really cool colors, like purple and yellow or blue and orange. That'd look so great."

"Hey, I knew you'd be a natural," said Kjerstina. "Those are complementary colors. They're opposites of each other on the color wheel." When Lauren looked at her blankly, she added, "I'll show you." Kjerstina pulled a book from the green bookshelf and carried it to the bed. She leafed through the pages and then held the book for Lauren to see. "See?" she asked.

Lauren took the book from her. The picture showed a circle like a pie cut into pieces. Each piece was a different color. "The colors across from each other in the wheel are

33

opposites. Red and green are opposites and see how cool they look together?" She waved her arm like a person on a game show displaying a valuable car.

"I really like the purple and yellow," said Lauren and looked up as a tall, seventeen-year-old girl hurried through the door with one towel wrapped around her hair and another wrapped around her body.

"Hi Charity," Lauren said and jumped up from the bed.

"Hey there, cuz," Charity said and gave Lauren a one-armed hug, keeping a firm grip on her towel with the other hand. "It's great to see you. I didn't think you were ever going to get here. Mom and Kjerstina left hours ago."

"The plane was late. It was almost too cloudy to land," explained Lauren. "I thought we might have to turn around and go back." She tried to stop the wistful tone from creeping into her voice.

"I'm glad the weather changed. What do you think of Stina's room? Isn't it funky?" asked Charity, pulling the towel off her head and grabbing the comb from Kjerstina's dresser. She started to pull it through her tangled hair.

"It's awesome," said Lauren.

"Hey, hurry up, Charity," interjected Kjerstina. "I want to show Lauren the surprise."

"Oh yeah," said Charity, her face brightening. "I forgot she doesn't know! Why don't you go out and start getting ready and I'll get dressed."

Kjerstina jumped up from the bed. "Just finish unpacking, Lauren. Yours is the bottom bunk and there are two empty drawers in the dresser," she said, pointing. "When you're done, come down to the kitchen. We should be ready by then."

34

"Okay," said Lauren. "But what is it? You've got to give me another hint. It can't be a big, golden soldier."

"No peeking out the window," Kjerstina yelled over her shoulder as she raced down the stairs.

"I'll be down in a minute," Charity called to her sister as she hurried to her own room.

"Make sure you comb your hair first," teased Kjerstina from the bottom of the stairs. "It looks hideous."

"Brat!" Charity yelled back.

Lauren wandered to the door and looked down the stairs. Kjerstina was already gone. She went back into the bedroom and pulled the door shut behind her. A minute later, she heard Charity run down the stairs. Silence fell over the house. Lauren sat down on the bed beside her suitcase and unzipped it. She took out the t-shirt wrapped picture and removed it from its covering. Then she reached into the suitcase pocket for the thumbtack. She hung the picture on the wall beneath the top bunk, so only she would see it. Her cousins knew about the painting, but she didn't want all of Kjerstina's friends to see it and ask about it.

Lauren learned a long time ago not to say anything about her mom's accident. It was normal to find kids that didn't have a dad for whatever reason, but every kid she'd ever met had a mom. And the worse thing was that they all felt sorry for Lauren when they found out. At least Charity and Kjerstina knew enough not to talk about it any more. Even Aunt April and Uncle Chris avoided the subject, unless they felt some adult-like duty to ask her how she was doing, *really* doing. Lauren hated it when they asked it like that. She never knew what to say.

She pulled the books out of the suitcase, opened a drawer and turned the suitcase upside down over it. Then she shut the drawer, put the books back into the suitcase and pushed it under her bed.

"Unpacking done," she said aloud and sighed. "Now lets see what this *amazing* surprise is that everyone's been talking about." She left the room, letting the door bang shut behind her.

Chapter Six

Lauren was halfway down the stairs when Kjerstina's voice yelled from the back door. "Lauren! Come outside! Come out through the kitchen."

"Here she is," said Aunt April when Lauren walked into the kitchen. "All unpacked?"

Lauren smiled. "Yes, I didn't bring much stuff," she added.

"Are you ready for your blindfold?" asked Aunt April and picked up a white dishcloth from the table.

"Blindfold?" asked Lauren, her voice sceptical. *They're carrying this surprise thing a little too far, aren't they?*

"You don't have to wear it if you don't want," Aunt April said and put the cloth down on the table. "Kjerstina just mentioned it, and well, you know how excited she gets about things."

"I don't mind," Lauren said and shrugged. "It doesn't matter."

"Well, let's go. You're ready to see what your surprise is anyway, aren't you?" Her voice sounded so hopeful that Lauren felt bad about not wanting to wear the blindfold.

"Am I ever, Aunt April," she replied. "But put the blindfold on me first, okay? Really. I'd rather have it on and make Stina happy." She held still as Aunt April tied the cloth around her eyes. The darkness felt good against her eyelids.

"Lauren!" Charity's voice came from outside.

"Okay, here we come," Aunt April called back. She guided Lauren to the back door. "Step over the threshold," she said and helped Lauren onto the porch. Then Aunt April moved behind her. "Are you ready?"

Lauren nodded. Aunt April fumbled with the knot, then the cloth fell free and the sun beamed onto Lauren's face. She put up her hand to shield her eyes from the brightness and gasped at what she saw.

Three horses stood in the backyard. Charity held the lead rope of the horse closest to Lauren, a tall leggy mare. The mare gleamed black with only a small white star in the middle of her forehead. Her coat glittered in the sunlight.

Next to the mare stood an athletic, dark brown gelding with a blaze running halfway down his face and a white snip on the end of his nose. He bobbed his head and stepped toward Lauren with his ears forward. Kjerstina held him back and a low nicker escaped from his throat.

The third horse shone a bright gold that perfectly accented his silky black mane, tail, legs, muzzle, and ears: a buckskin. A crescent shaped star sat exactly between his dark eyes and a pink sheet flopped around his neck. Kjerstina stood proudly between the two geldings, a lead rope in each hand. It took Lauren a moment to register that Kjerstina and Charity were laughing at the shocked expression on her face.

"You look so surprised! I knew you would be," exclaimed Kjerstina and bounced up and down for a moment. "Come and meet our new project. Mom and Dad got them for us this spring. Aren't they awesome? It's

been absolutely terrible keeping it a secret from you. I wanted to phone you a thousand, million, billion times!"

Charity led her black mare forward. "This is Orion. Isn't she the greatest?"

"She's amazing."

"I absolutely adore her. She's my new best friend," said Charity tenderly. She leaned into Orion's shoulder. "Come and say 'hi'."

Lauren tore her eyes from the beautiful horse to walk down the steps. The last thing she wanted to do was embarrass herself by tripping on the steps and falling. She couldn't believe this was happening! It was like a dream, the best possible, imaginable dream come true! Orion put her head down and sniffed at Lauren, then snorted, spraying Charity and Lauren with tiny wet flecks.

Charity laughed. "She likes you," she said to Lauren. "I can tell. She doesn't snot on just anybody."

"Yes, she does," argued Kjerstina. "She does it all the time."

Lauren stroked the velvet neck. "She's beautiful. You're so lucky."

"She's a great jumper too. I'll show you later. We have some practice jumps set up in the back."

"That's enough time with Orion," said Kjerstina. "Come see Coyote." She pulled her horse forward a couple steps. "He's an Anglo-Arab."

"What's that?" asked Lauren, turning toward the gelding.

"It's just a fancy way of saying he's an Arabian/ Thoroughbred cross," said Kjerstina, shrugging her shoulders.

"He's such a cool color, like shiny chocolate," said Lauren reaching out to smooth Coyote's mane.

40

"He's a liver chestnut," said Kjerstina and made a face. "I know it sounds gross. They should have called it a midnight chestnut or coffee chestnut or something like that. Almost anything is better than *liver* chestnut."

"The white spot on his nose is adorable and his eyes are so big and brown," said Lauren as she admired the finely etched head and large expressive eyes.

"Yeah," said Kjerstina. "He has an Arabian face. And he doesn't snot on people!"

"Yes, he does," disagreed Charity.

"Who's this?" asked Lauren, turning to the buckskin gelding. She touched the soft black muzzle. "Is he Aunt April's?" The gelding sniffed at Lauren's hand, then pointed his ears forward, whinnied low in his throat and lowered his head so she could stroke his golden face.

"No," said Kjerstina. Her voice sounded strained to Lauren and she turned to look at her cousin. Kjerstina's face was contorted and Lauren realized she was trying not to grin.

"Is he Uncle Chris'?" Lauren asked with a puzzled voice.

"No," said Kjerstina and shut her mouth tightly.

Then Aunt April's voice came quietly from behind Lauren. "He's yours, Lauren."

"What?" Lauren couldn't believe her ears. "Mine? Really? He can't be! *Mine*?"

Kjerstina and Charity laughed. "Yeah, he's yours," said Kjerstina. "All yours. Your dad sent the money to buy him!"

Lauren didn't know what to say. Words didn't seem enough. With a trembling hand she took the lead rope that Kjerstina offered.

"I knew you'd like him," said Charity. "His name is

41

Trooper and he's a Thoroughbred/Morgan cross. He's an awesome jumper and he's won a ton of ribbons. He's twenty-four years old, but he doesn't look it, does he?"

"He's wonderful. Totally perfect," breathed Lauren. She leaned forward and rested her forehead against Trooper's face. She drew a deep breath. "He smells nice too," she said after pulling away. Trooper whinnied and nuzzled her with his nose and Lauren leaned back into him.

"Do you want to go for a ride?" asked Charity.

"I'd love to!" said Lauren, still breathless with the wonder of having her own horse. "Can we? Are we allowed?"

Kjerstina laughed. "Of course we can. That's what the horses are here for. Come on." She led Coyote toward the gate to the paddock and Charity fell in behind her, leading Orion.

"Wait a minute, Lauren," said Aunt April. She walked to Trooper and started to untie the sheet that was hanging around his neck.

"What's the sheet for?" asked Lauren.

Aunt April glanced at her daughters, leading their horses away. "That's Stina's attempt at a bow, I'm afraid," she whispered as she pulled the sheet from around Trooper's neck.

Unexpectedly, Lauren felt the prickle of tears in her eyes. She blinked quickly to chase them away. "Thank you so much, Aunt April," she choked. "For everything." She flung her arms around her aunt's ample waist.

Aunt April's arms closed warm and soft around Lauren's shoulders. "You're very welcome, sweetheart. You know we love you."

"I love you too," said Lauren. "I can't believe you would do all this for me."

42

"Your dad is the main one. We're only supplying the place for Trooper to live," said Aunt April.

Lauren pulled away. "Can you hold him for a minute? I have to phone Dad. I can't wait until tonight."

"Sure, Honey."

But all Lauren got was the answering machine. *He's out catching the stalker,* she thought after leaving a quick message. *He'll call tonight and I'll tell him how wonderful he is. Tell him how useless his hint was. And tell him all about Trooper.*

She bounded back down the back porch stairs and took the lead rope from Aunt April. "Thanks, Aunt April. Trooper, we're going to have a wonderful time this summer," she said to the buckskin and turned toward the barn. Trooper nickered and nuzzled her with his nose as they walked. Charity and Kjerstina stood outside the new barn with their horses, waiting for her.

It's like a dream come true, Lauren thought. *I guess I am glad I came to Misty Lake. Amazingly glad. Stina's right. It's going to be the most perfect summer ever.*

Chapter Seven

The girls tied the horses to rings in the wall outside the new barn and Lauren followed Kjerstina and Charity inside. They walked past four roomy stalls, two on each side of the barn aisle. There were two rooms on the end.

"That's where we keep the grain and supplements," Kjerstina said motioning toward the door to the left. She opened the door to the right and walked into a tack room. It still smelled of new wood. Four saddles stood on saddle racks against the far wall and bridles hung on hooks shaped like horseshoes.

"The western saddle is yours to use for now," said Charity. "We got it from the people that used to own Trooper, so it fits him perfectly. My saddle is this dark brown one. It's a jumping saddle and Kjerstina's is the black dressage saddle. The black jumping saddle is for Trooper too, but Mom thought it would be better if you learned to ride with the western saddle. It's harder to fall off with it."

"What's dressage?" asked Lauren, running her hand over Kjerstina's sleek black saddle.

"It's a sport where the horse and rider communicate with each other so well that they can do lots of hard things, like trot sideways and canter in one spot, and stuff like that," said Kjerstina. "I'll show you a video when we go back to the house, if you want. I can't do it very well yet, but it's amazing what the real professionals can do. Their horses are so graceful they look like swans floating on air. I'm trying to get good enough to enter the beginner classes in the fair this year. My riding instructor says that I'm a quick learner and Coyote seems to be catching on fast, so there's a chance."

"When's the fair? Maybe I'll still be here then," said Lauren. "I'd love to cheer you on."

"You might be here. It's in August," said Charity, then she added, "Hey, you should think of entering Trooper in some of the classes. He's a great jumper. I'm going to be entering Orion too."

"That would be fun," said Lauren. Her heart raced as she thought of Trooper flying through the air over jump after jump with her on his back. "But I've never ridden before," she added. "What if I can't do it?"

"You can take lessons with us," suggested Charity. "Our instructor will let you know if you're ready in time. They have lots of beginner classes at the fair."

"Awesome!" said Lauren. She pulled the western saddle and blanket from the saddle rack and lugged them outside to the horses. Charity grabbed Trooper's bridle from the hook.

First, Charity and Kjerstina showed Lauren how to groom Trooper and then how to tack him up. Then they took the saddle and bridle off again and Lauren saddled Trooper by herself as they gave her pointers. Charity showed her how to pick up Trooper's feet and clean his hooves, and Kjerstina showed her how Trooper especially liked his forehead scratched. She laughed as she rumpled his forelock.

45

"He looks like a punk rocker now," Kjerstina said, when Trooper's forelock was sticking out all over the place. Then she smoothed his hair down again and tucked it under the brow band of his bridle.

"Okay," said Charity as she gave Trooper a final pat on the shoulder. "We'll saddle Orion and Coyote in a minute. First, I'll show you what to do when you're riding him and then you can ride around a bit while we're getting our horses ready."

Charity took Trooper's reins in one hand and stood in the left stirrup, then she swung her leg over his back. Trooper stood still as she settled into the saddle. Charity shifted her weight and pulled gently back on the reins.

"Back," she said to the gelding and Trooper stepped back from the barn. She laid the reins against the right side of his neck and Trooper turned to the left, away from the pressure of the reins.

As Charity rode the buckskin around the field, she explained to Lauren what she was doing. "When I want him to stop, I do more than pull back on the reins. I say 'whoa' too, and settle back in the saddle a bit. He can feel the shift of my weight and knows that I want him to stop. He's a really smart horse. When I want him to go, I squeeze with my lower legs and lean forward just a tiny bit. I can say 'walk on' or 'trot' too. He knows all the voice commands. When you start riding with the jumping saddle, some of the reining will be different, but almost everything else will be the same."

When Lauren felt she was ready, Charity held Trooper by the bridle and Lauren grabbed the stirrup. She took a deep breath, stood in the stirrup, swung her leg over and plopped down hard in the saddle. Trooper turned his head and looked at her and Lauren was sure he was smiling at her clumsiness.

Lauren took another deep breath, trying to calm her pounding heart. She was riding! Actually riding a horse. And a beautiful horse at that. His long black mane and tail accented his golden coat perfectly. She gathered the reins and Charity let go of Trooper's bridle. Lauren raised the reins and shook them. Trooper didn't move.

"Remember, you have to squeeze your calves against his sides and say 'walk on,'" reminded Kjerstina.

"Walk on," said Lauren in a small voice and squeezed slightly. Trooper took a step forward and Lauren grabbed for the saddle horn.

"He'll be fine," said Charity. "You don't need to hold onto the horn."

Lauren slowly released the saddle horn. "How do I stay on then?" she asked.

"Just stay balanced in the saddle. He's not going to run unless you ask him to," said Charity.

"Okay," Lauren breathed and sat up straight. Trooper stepped across the field in slow, measured steps, as if he knew it was her first ride. When they reached the end of the pasture, Lauren laid the reins across the left side of his neck like Charity had done. Trooper made a quick right. Then Lauren turned him the other way.

"That's it. Practice makes perfect," called Charity.

"We're going to get Orion and Coyote ready now," yelled Kjerstina.

"Okay," said Lauren and turned Trooper toward the barn again. She wove him left and right, then said "Whoa," shifted her weight and pulled back on the reins. She pulled too hard and Trooper tossed his head.

"Sorry," said Lauren and glanced at the barn. She was

glad Charity and Kjerstina were inside and hadn't seen. Lauren asked Trooper to walk again, then stopped him, but this time she used less pressure on the bit. He stopped without tossing his head and Lauren patted him on the neck.

"You are so amazing, Trooper," whispered Lauren to the horse. She smiled when he turned his head slightly and looked back at her.

His mane is like ebony silk, she thought as she ran her free hand through the thick black hair. *And he's so gentle that I don't feel scared at all anymore.* She leaned forward in the saddle and kissed the top of his neck. "I still can't believe you're mine. All mine and no one else's. It's so weird. And so wonderful! How could Dad keep you a secret?"

Lauren turned Trooper toward the bottom of the pasture. His hooves thudded rhythmically on the soft grass and Lauren revelled in the sway of his body as he walked. When they reached the fence she turned him around.

Charity and Kjerstina were riding toward her. Their horses shone like satin in the sunlight. The green field and wooden fences and trees and mountains behind were like something from a painting. Lauren smiled at her cousins as they approached.

"You still look like you're in shock," laughed Kjerstina.

All Lauren could do was nod.

Chapter Eight

"We're going to take the short trail through the woods. It goes to this really cool clearing," said Kjerstina reining Coyote beside Trooper. "We can't go far because we have to be back in a couple hours for dinner, but you'll like it. Trooper likes it there too."

"Yeah," added Charity. "We took him there a few days ago when he needed some exercise."

"It sounds wonderful," replied Lauren.

And it was wonderful. They rode along the road for a short distance, turned the horses into a gap in the trees and walked single file down the well-worn trail. Huge trees stretched up out of sight all around them, some with moss and ferns hanging from their lower branches like miniature gardens high in the air. The forest floor was brushy and wherever there was a patch of sunlight, wild pink roses and golden salmonberries glowed in the light. Kjerstina and Charity talked softly and sometimes Kjerstina even sang, but the sound didn't seem to carry far. The thick clumps of vegetation muffled the noises. Still, between two of Kjerstina's songs, Lauren heard a branch break in the distance.

"There are wild animals around here, aren't there?"

50

Lauren asked, suddenly remembering a story Kjerstina told her last summer about a black bear coming into their front yard.

"Oh yes," replied Kjerstina. "There's lots. Bears and wolves and moose."

"That's why we make so much noise," explained Charity. "So they hear us and run away. Most wild animals are afraid of people."

"Or at least that's what we hope," said Kjerstina with a mischievous glint in her eyes. Then she laughed. "Don't look so worried, Lauren. I was just bugging you!"

"I wasn't worried," Lauren lied.

"Stina, don't be so mean," said Charity, her voice irritated. She turned in her saddle to look back at Lauren. "The horses can sense if a bear is near. You just have to trust Trooper."

"He'll neigh if he senses a bear?" asked Lauren hopefully.

"No, but he'll act scared and jumpy or maybe even try to run home. And if he points his ears and acts interested in something, you should always pay attention."

"And hold on tight because something's going to jump out at you," added Kjerstina, then snapped her mouth shut when both Charity and Lauren threw her black looks.

"It just means he's checking things out," added Charity. "Probably just a dog or cat or the wind moving the leaves, but it's always good to be aware. That's all."

"Okay," said Lauren and locked her eyes onto Trooper's ears. He seemed to be relaxed, as if he were enjoying their outing.

"Sorry, Lauren," added Kjerstina, her voice subdued now. "Really, we hardly ever see any wild animals. I wish we'd see more but they always hear us and run away be-

51

fore we even know they're there. I saw a couple of deer one day, but that's all."

"It's okay," said Lauren, accepting her apology. Kjerstina's teasing could be irritating sometimes, but she wasn't mean. Lauren leaned forward and stroked Trooper's neck.

"Hey look, we're almost there," said Charity and asked Orion to trot. Kjerstina immediately urged Coyote forward. Lauren straightened in the saddle. She could tell that Trooper wanted to follow them, so she took a deep breath, squeezed her calves against his sides and said "trot."

Trooper sprang forward. Lauren bounced in the saddle as the gelding tried to catch up to the other two horses. When she started to slip to the side, she grabbed for the saddle horn. "Whoa," she yelled. She wanted to pull back on the reins but she knew she would fall if she let go of the saddle, so she just hung on as tight as she could. Trooper slowed a little, but didn't stop trotting. Lauren felt herself slip a little more to the side, then a little more.

Finally, Trooper caught up to Orion and Coyote and they all stopped. Lauren breathed heavily as she pulled herself straight in the saddle. "Wow," she said to her cousins. "That was scary."

"Hey, you did better than I did the first time," said Kjerstina enthusiastically. "I fell off, but then Coyote isn't as steady as Trooper. When I started to slip, he jumped sideways." Kjerstina laughed and patted the dark brown neck. "I've forgiven him though. It was a long way down, but it didn't hurt as bad as I thought it would."

"Come on," urged Charity. "We're going to be late getting home if we don't hurry." She turned Orion off the main trail. The new trail was narrow and faint and not very long. After a few minutes, they rode into a grassy glade surrounded by a thick stand of brush and trees. A tiny pool of water bubbled up from the ground in the center of the clearing and trickled off to one side.

"Isn't it cool?" said Charity dismounting. "An underground spring pops up here. The water is warm too."

"Not many people know about it. We learned about it from Mom. She discovered it when she was a kid," said Kjerstina.

Lauren dismounted and led Trooper toward the tiny spring. She knelt and tentatively touched the water. The current rising from the ground made the warm water swirl and bubble around her hand. *It's just like a miniature hot tub,* thought Lauren. Trooper lowered his head beside her and drank from the pool.

"See. He doesn't even hesitate," said Kjerstina in amazement. "He's so cool. Orion and Coyote won't have anything to do with the spring." To prove her point, she tried to ride Coyote toward the water. Coyote danced to the side and tossed his head. Kjerstina slipped from his back and led him toward the pool. "He's such a big baby," she said. "As long as I go first, he'll follow. He thinks that if there are any big scary monsters hiding in that tiny pool waiting to jump out, they'll get me first and he can run away."

Lauren giggled as Coyote walked gingerly behind Kjerstina, all his attention on the tiny pool of water. "I'm glad Trooper's sensible."

"Yeah, you're lucky."

Charity joined them, Orion's bridle swinging in her hand. Orion grazed at the edge of the clearing, her head free.

"Won't she run away?" asked Lauren, amazed.

"No, she won't leave the other horses." Charity sat on the soft herbs beside her sister and cousin. "So now tell us, Lauren. We've been dying to know what's been happening."

"Yeah, now that we've got you alone, the questioning begins," teased Kjerstina. "We overheard part of a phone conversation Mom had with Uncle Alan and all we know is that you're running from something. It's not the law, is it? Mom seemed shocked."

"No, I didn't break the law," said Lauren and smiled at Kjerstina's faked sigh of relief. "Really, its not that big a deal. Someone's been following me, that's all. Someone in a blue car. And he took some pictures of me."

"What? Who's taking pictures of you?" asked Kjerstina, sounding genuinely confused.

"Start at the beginning," said Charity. "Tell us the whole story, okay?"

Lauren started with the first time she noticed the blue car. As she told her cousins what happened, she was surprised at how scary it sounded. Especially the part about the man's hands rising up and pointing the camera toward her, his finger twitching over the button as he took her picture.

"That's horrible! I'm so glad Sweetie was with you. Do you have any idea who it was?" Charity asked when Lauren finished her story.

"No."

Charity and Kjerstina looked at each other. Then Kjerstina spoke. "Can you keep a secret?" When Lauren nodded, she continued, "We think Mom and Uncle Alan know who it is."

"What?"

"It was just something Mom said on the phone. As if

55

your dad guessed who was following you. I can't remember her exact words, but it was something like 'Are you sure? After all these years away? After everything that happened?' Or something like that."

An cold hand brushed down Lauren's spine. "I wonder… one thing makes sense now," she said, the words slow and thoughtful. "Dad asked me if Sweetie knew the person. He seemed to think it was important that Sweetie noticed Big Hat sitting there. And maybe it was."

"Do you think she did know who it was?" asked Kjerstina.

Lauren sighed. "I don't know now. She was curious. But maybe she just saw that Big Hat was watching us or noticed him taking our picture. Dogs are sensitive that way, right? Maybe she felt threatened or somehow knew Big Hat was after me."

Silence filled the glade. Lauren trailed her hand through the water, deep in thought.

"The thing I wonder is, if Mom and Uncle Alan suspect they know who's been following you…" said Kjerstina.

"Why would they keep it a secret from you?" finished Charity.

Lauren looked up and shook her head. "I don't know." Trooper moved to stand over her and lowered his head. Lauren reached to stroke his cheek. *Doesn't my dad trust me? Is he in trouble? In danger?*

"We should be going home," Charity said, interrupting Lauren's thoughts. "I don't want to be late on our first ride with Lauren. Mom won't let us out tomorrow if we're late."

"Okay, but let's not trot," said Lauren.

"It's not that hard," replied Charity, climbing to her feet. "You just have to grip with your knees. But not too

56

tight or you kind of pop up like a cork. You can stand in the stirrups too or you can post, like we do. Here. I'll show you." She slipped the bridle onto Orion's fine head and settled into the saddle. She urged the black mare into a trot and circled the clearing, standing in the stirrups on every second step and sinking back to the saddle seat in between.

"Let me try it before we go, okay?" asked Lauren, still unsure. She scrambled into Trooper's saddle and urged the gelding into a walk. Then, keeping her hands low as she had seen Charity do, she said "trot." Trooper broke into a trot and Lauren grabbed for the saddle horn again.

"Keep your heels down when you stand in the stirrups," suggested Kjerstina. "It will help you stay balanced."

"O...o...k...kay," stammered Lauren as she bounced. Trooper trotted slowly around the perimeter of the clearing, hesitating only to step carefully over the cooling runoff from the underground spring. He seemed to instinctively know he shouldn't jump over the stream of cooling water. After a couple of turns around the clearing, Lauren's grip loosened on the saddle horn and her seat became steadier. Finally she pulled Trooper to a halt.

"Okay," she said, her voice relieved. "I think I can do this. But stop if I yell 'Whoa,' all right?"

They didn't take long to get home. When they trotted down the driveway, Aunt April was waiting for them. "I was getting worried about you," she said.

"We're not that late, Mom," said Kjerstina and looked at Lauren with fake exasperation. "Only a couple of minutes."

"How was the ride?" Aunt April asked and reached to stroke Trooper's face.

"It was wonderful. And Trooper's so amazing," said Lauren. "I love him already." Trooper turned his head and snuffled at Lauren's foot. "He's the perfect horse," she added.

"Well, not perfect," said Aunt April.

"No, not perfect," confirmed Kjerstina. "He has one major and very irritating flaw."

"As we found out the first night we got him here," said Charity.

"What?"

Aunt April smiled. "His previous owners warned us he's an escape artist. He can untie almost any knot or undo almost any latch if you give him enough time."

"I'll tie double knots whenever I tie him up," promised Lauren.

"We do too. *Now*," said Kjerstina. "And we never forget to use the special latches they gave us anymore either."

"We forgot to put them on the first night we brought him home and the next morning he was grazing in Mom's garden," said Charity, trying to hide a smile.

"I was *not* impressed," said Aunt April. "But then he looked at me with those big brown eyes and I remembered how trustworthy he is and how many kids he's taught to ride, so he got to stay."

"But it was so sad. All those baby carrots that were waiting to be thinned, all those tiny peas and beets and beans that needed to be weeded. I'm going to miss spending hours and hours working so much," said Kjerstina, trying not to laugh.

Aunt April looked at her disapprovingly, but then decided to ignore her comment. "They said he's especially good at escaping and they heard that he once saved his own life by opening his stall door."

58

"Wow!" exclaimed Lauren. "What happened? Was there a fire?"

"I'm not sure what happened. It was years ago, when he was young. All they knew was Trooper escaped. There were rumors that the other animals died."

"That's so sad," said Lauren and a strange shiver ran down her spine.

"That *is* way too sad," said Kjerstina. "Lets not think about it anymore."

"Yeah," added Charity. "I'm just glad Trooper made it out."

"Well, dinner's almost ready, and since the horses around here eat before the humans, you better go take care of them," said Aunt April. She patted Trooper one more time on the neck and turned toward the house.

Lauren rode Trooper toward the barn behind her cousins. At the gate, she dismounted and looked at the chain and clip hanging there. "This is how they keep you in now, is it, Troops?" she said to the gelding and put the chain around the gatepost. It took a moment to figure out the clip. When she finally had it in place, she led Trooper toward the barn.

"I'm so glad you were able to escape, Trooper," she crooned as they walked. "And, I know I shouldn't be, but I'm glad you ate Aunt April's garden. Since I have to stay all summer, she probably would've asked me to weed too."

Chapter Nine

Lauren lingered in the barn after Charity and Kjerstina went back to the house. She couldn't bear leaving Trooper yet. The wonder of owning a horse, a beautiful golden horse, was finally starting to sink in. She swept the body brush over his glistening coat, breathed in his horsey scent, and listened to the chewing sounds he made as he ate his oats. The sounds were relaxing and soon Lauren found her thoughts returning to what she had learned from Charity and Kjerstina.

"Do you think my dad really knows who was following me, Trooper?" she asked. It was nice to talk to someone even if he couldn't reply or understand. "It makes sense in a way, because Sweetie did seem to notice Big Hat for no reason. Charity and Stina think he knows. But he's never kept important secrets from me before. I can't believe he would just send me away and not tell me. Except for you, he's never, ever kept secrets from me."

But is that true? How can I know for sure? The question leaped unbidden into her mind. She picked up a large toothed comb and moved behind Trooper to comb his tail. He looked back at her and nickered, then turned back to his oats.

"I'm going to ask him tonight," Lauren said to the

buckskin gelding. "Maybe he's just keeping it a secret because he doesn't want me to worry, but if he knows I know that he thinks he knows who it is, he'll realize I'm already worried and thinking about it and then maybe he'll tell me."

She finished combing out Trooper's tail and leaned on his hindquarters for a moment. "Are you confused yet Trooper? I know I am. That didn't make any sense to me either, and I'm the one who said it."

Lauren moved to Trooper's head and combed his forelock. "You are so beautiful," she whispered to the golden gelding. "My very own horse. I still can't believe it." She kissed Trooper on the nose.

"Lauren," Kjerstina's voice came from outside the barn. "Dinner's ready."

"Coming," called Lauren. She gave Trooper one more hug, then picked up the brushes and walked out of the stall.

"Remember the special clip for his door," said Kjerstina, stepping inside the barn. Uncle Chris was right behind her.

"Hey, Lauren," he said in his cheerful voice. "Long time, no see."

"Hey, Uncle Chris."

"Come give your favorite uncle a hug," he said and held his arms out.

"But he's not here," said Lauren, teasing him. "How about I give you a hug instead, Uncle Chris?" She rushed into his arms.

"Cheeky as ever," said Uncle Chris and squeezed her back. "But you can't fool me. I know I'm your favorite uncle."

"You're my *only* uncle." Lauren's voice was muffled by his hug.

61

"Aha. My point exactly." He reached to tickle her on the ribs and Lauren squirmed out of his embrace.

"I'm too old to be tickled now, Uncle Chris," she informed him.

A look of dismay crossed his face. "Oh, that's right. Another birthday coming up. What are you now? Eighteen? Nineteen?"

"No! Thirteen."

"Oh, well I guess you're not too old then," he added and grinned.

Kjerstina groaned beside Lauren. "You walked right into that one," she said. "Hey, come over here. I'll show you how to use the clip for Trooper's door. See? It goes on like a padlock, except it doesn't lock."

"Thanks, Stina," said Lauren, even though she'd already figured it out at the gate.

Kjerstina smiled. "No prob," she said as they walked toward the door where Uncle Chris waited for them. "I'm so glad you're staying all summer. We're going to have tons of fun, you know."

"I know," said Lauren. "It's going to be the best summer ever."

"What do you want to do for your birthday?" asked Uncle Chris, as they left the barn.

"I'm going back home for my party. Dad said he's coming to pick me up."

"But that doesn't mean you can't have two birthday parties."

"Oh, lets do something fun!" exclaimed Kjerstina. "We could go swimming at the lake. And have tons of cake and other good stuff to eat."

"And go hiking and canoeing," added Lauren. She smiled. Actually, it didn't sound half bad.

Dinner was roast chicken, and Lauren had just finished dishing up her plate when the phone rang. Uncle Chris didn't want anyone to answer, but Aunt April jumped up anyway. "It could be Alan," she flung back over her shoulder as she hurried into the kitchen.

It was. Aunt April talked to him for a minute, telling him about Lauren's shocked face when she first saw the horses, then she called to Lauren.

"Why don't you run upstairs and talk on the phone in our bedroom," she suggested. "I'll hang up here when you've picked up."

"Thanks," said Lauren and pushed her chair back. She ran up the stairs two at a time. When she picked up the phone she was breathing heavily.

"Hi, Dad," she said.

"Hi, Kiddo." He sounded happy to hear her. Lauren heard the soft click as Aunt April hung up the phone downstairs.

"You miss me?" she asked.

"More than you'll ever know. I hear you were surprised. I thought you'd guess after my hint."

"Soldier? What kind of hint was that? Hmmm. Oh, I know. A *terrible* hint."

They talked for a few minutes about Trooper and how wonderful he was, about Lauren's first ride and the hidden springs, Trooper's skill in escaping and the fate of Aunt April's garden. Then the conversation moved to the stalker. Had he found out who it was? He hadn't. Had he seen the car again? No. What had the police said? They hadn't contacted him yet. Why hadn't he called them? He was busy. This last answer sparked the courage in Lauren to ask the question she really wanted to ask. "Do you know who the person is, Dad?"

63

There was stunned silence on the phone.

"Dad? Are you still there?"

"Yes. What makes you think I know who it is?"

He's trying to distract me, realized Lauren. "Do you?" she asked again, not letting him sidetrack her.

"Oh, I'm sorry, Lauren," he said, his voice hurried. "I forgot I have an appointment. I don't have time to talk about it right now, but we can talk about it another time, okay?"

Lauren was speechless. Her dad had never brushed her off before. Kjerstina and Charity were right. He did know who it was. Or he at least suspected. He didn't want to lie to her, but he wasn't going to tell her either.

"I'll call you tomorrow, okay, Kiddo? Bye now." There was a soft click.

"Dad?"

No answer. He was gone.

He didn't even wait for me to say goodbye, Lauren realized in shock. *What is going on?*

Chapter Ten

The next night he called but could only talk for a minute. Then he didn't call for two nights after that. When Lauren phoned him, there was no answer. She left messages on his machine, but even then he took three days before he phoned back. And again, he didn't have time to talk. Lauren thought of approaching Aunt April and asking her whom she thought the stranger was, but then decided against it. She didn't want to get Aunt April in trouble with her dad and she knew her aunt probably wouldn't tell her anyway. If it hadn't been for Trooper and the time they spent together, Lauren was sure she would've gone insane with worry and frustration. Grown-ups could be so irritating!

She rode Trooper with Charity and Kjerstina every day, even when it rained. As her skill increased, the three girls rode farther and farther. They discovered new trails through the woods, creeks that bubbled magically from the undergrowth, and a hidden meadow along the shore of one of the small crystal clear lakes near the larger Misty Lake.

Lauren took a riding lesson with Lisa, her cousins' riding instructor, and was happy to hear that Lisa thought she was a natural rider. After the lesson, she was so excited she couldn't wait to talk to her dad. But all she got was the answering machine. Again.

After Lauren had been in Misty Lake for almost two weeks, Aunt April drove her to the local tack store while Charity and Kjerstina were visiting friends. Lauren bought hoof glitter and some spray that promised to add super shine to a horse's mane and tail. When she got back, Lauren ran to the barn to try the new purchases on Trooper. After an enjoyable hour experimenting in the barn, she led Trooper into the sunlight.

"Wow," she whispered when the sun caught Trooper's mane and tail. The long hair glistened midnight blue. His hooves shone in the light like rainbows. Lauren turned him loose in the paddock and Trooper pranced across the grass. Lauren ran after him, exalting in the wind in her face. She spun in a circle in the middle of the field and fell backwards, her face to the sky.

Trooper walked up to her and snorted into her face. Lauren couldn't stop from laughing out loud. "It's a glorious day, isn't it?" she said to the buckskin. "We should go for a ride."

Lauren jumped to her feet and clipped the lead rope back onto Trooper's halter. She led him back to the barn and tied him with a double knot, then ran to the house.

"Aunt April, is it okay if I go riding by myself?" she asked hopefully.

Her aunt turned from the sink where she was washing dishes. "Where do you want to go?" she asked. "I wouldn't like you to go too far if you're going to be alone."

"Can I go to the little warm spring in the woods? That's not too far, and I promise I won't be gone long," Lauren replied.

"Okay," agreed Aunt April. "But be back before six. That's an hour and a half."

"Thanks, Aunt April," said Lauren. She flashed a smile at her aunt before racing out the door and back to the barn.

In a few minutes, Trooper was saddled and bridled. Lauren led him to the gate and undid the special chain and clip. She took him through and latched the gate, then climbed into the saddle.

"Let's go, boy," she said in an excited voice and squeezed Trooper's sides. This was the first time Lauren had been riding by herself and she was looking forward to it. There was no one to remind her of how elusive her dad was being, no one to theorize on what was happening back home. Lauren didn't blame Charity and Kjerstina. She knew they couldn't help it. She knew her cousins just thought of the whole situation as an intriguing mystery to be solved. But it hurt Lauren to think of how her dad was avoiding her.

I'm just going to have fun and forget about Dad for the rest of the day, she decided and patted Trooper on his neck. Trooper was excited to be out and stepped forward eagerly. Soon they came to the break in the trees where the trail started and Lauren turned Trooper into the woods.

The whole world changed when they stepped into the forest. Almost immediately the sound of traffic from the road was shut out. It was so quiet. So still. Lauren knew she should probably make some noise to alert any wild animals to their presence, but she couldn't stand the thought of breaking the peaceful atmosphere. The needles strewn on the trail muffled Trooper's glittering hooves and Lauren noticed that even the sound of their breathing was easy to hear. *I'll let Trooper take care of me*, she decided. *He'll keep me safe.*

Soon they came to where the tiny trail to the warm spring branched off the main trail. Lauren turned Trooper toward the spring. In the clearing, she slipped from the saddle and pulled Trooper's reins over his head. Then she sat down and removed her shoes and socks. The warm bubbling water felt so good on her feet. Lauren wished the pool was big enough that she could just climb in. She needed to relax. All this stuff with her dad was driving her nuts.

"But I decided not to think about that, didn't I?" she said to her horse. Trooper pulled on the reins in her hand and Lauren turned to look at him. "Hey boy, what's up? You don't want to stand around and wait for me?" Trooper tugged again and nickered to Lauren.

"Okay, okay," she finally said. Reluctantly, she pulled her feet from the water. "We'll go do something fun. I don't need to relax anyway. I just need to toughen up." Trooper nickered again and Lauren laughed. "You're not supposed to agree," she protested.

When she was securely in the saddle, she directed Trooper back the way they had come. They reached the main trail again and Lauren reined the horse to the left, away from Aunt April's house. "Let's go exploring a bit, okay, buddy?" she said.

Past the turnoff to the spring, the trail wasn't as well developed. It looked as if it was only used by wild animals, all of which were shorter than Trooper, and Lauren kept having to push branches out of her way. After a stretch of ducking branches and pulling fir and pine twigs from her hair, Lauren was relieved when the trail began to climb higher. She clung to the saddle as Trooper lurched higher and higher up the rocky hillside. The trees grew

68

farther apart on the hillside, and the agile gelding wove between the trunks with ease. When they reached a flat place, Lauren reined him around to look back the way they had come.

The view was breathtaking. Multiple greens lay over the land like a carpet, dotted with small topaz and aquamarine lakes. The larger Misty Lake lay behind them like a giant sapphire. From this height, she could see why it was called Misty Lake. A thin, white veil wisped around the edge of the gigantic lake.

"Wow," Lauren whispered. She looked to where she expected her aunt and uncle's house to be, but couldn't see it. They weren't high enough to see the things closer to the foot of the mountain. "Let's go higher, Trooper," she said and turned him away from the beautiful scene. They climbed until they hit a rock wall. Lauren directed Trooper along the cliff, searching for a path they could use to climb higher. The trail they had been following was long gone.

We're bushwhacking, thought Lauren, thinking of a phrase her Uncle Chris used that she always thought was funny. *I'm a bushwhacker. Just wait until I tell Dad.*

As they rode along the bottom of the rock wall, Lauren noticed they were being forced to go downhill. Lauren thought of turning Trooper around, but she didn't want to go back yet. There was still time before her hour and a half was up.

"I love exploring," she said aloud to the buckskin gelding. Trooper looked back at her and nickered. "You too?" asked Lauren and leaned forward to pat his neck. Again she marvelled that she was riding her very own horse, his step eager and springy, his ears forward and eyes bright. Trooper was the perfect horse for her.

When Trooper first turned away from the rock wall to scoot down a steep section, Lauren was surprised. She hadn't asked him to turn, and wondered if she should rein him back the way they had come. The forests were endless and they could easily get lost. She looked back to see the iron gray rock bluff behind her.

As long as I can see that, I'm okay, she reasoned. *And Trooper seems to know exactly where he's going. I wonder if he's been here before?* The gelding was almost trotting now. Lauren clutched the reins a little tighter and Trooper slid down another short, steep section.

Lauren pulled him to a stop. They were on an overgrown road. The little hill Trooper had slid down was the upper embankment.

"Where are we, boy?" she asked and wished he could answer her. The road was overgrown with bushes and young saplings. Lauren looked both ways. The brushy road twisted out of sight in both directions.

"Let's go to the right, Troops. I'm sure it'll come out at the road that goes in front of Aunt April's if we do," said Lauren. She glanced at her wristwatch. "It's probably faster than going back, and we've got to hurry now if we want to make it in time. She reined Trooper to the right and squeezed her calves against his side, but Trooper turned to the left and strode along the overgrown road.

"Whoa," Lauren said and pulled back on the reins. Trooper stopped and Lauren laid the reins against his neck to turn him around. But instead of turning back the way he came, Trooper turned in a complete circle. He took two steps forward before Lauren stopped him again.

"What are you doing, Trooper?" she asked, exasperated. "I don't want to go this way. We don't have time to explore any more. Aunt April's going to be worried if we're late." She tried to turn him, but again Trooper turned in a complete circle. And again. Now they were even farther along the overgrown road, in the wrong direction.

"Trooper," she said, her voice on the edge of panic. "Turn around. This isn't the right way!" She tried turning the horse again and, once more, he slowly and deliberately turned in a complete circle and eagerly stepped in the wrong direction.

She remembered what Lisa said about being the boss of the horse. Up until now, Trooper had been perfect. He had never tried to take advantage of her inexperience. *I need to be firm*, she remembered, *and gentle at the same time.*

She turned Trooper toward Aunt April's house and, when he kept turning in a full circle, she didn't stop him. Instead she kept turning him. They spun in circles in the middle of the road until Lauren grew dizzy and Trooper finally stopped, facing the right direction.

"Good boy," said Lauren and Trooper snorted in resignation. She squeezed his sides and he reluctantly stepped forward. "Good boy," Lauren repeated and stroked him. Lisa had said to reward the horse when he did the right thing.

After a few steps, Trooper regained his good temper and Lauren relaxed a bit. Trooper seemed to forget their disagreement and stepped forward with a springy step and ears perked forward. He was eager to please her again, so Lauren let him trot along the clearer sections of the brushy road. The fresh breeze against her face helped to blow away some of her confusion. They had only gone a short distance when Lauren heard the sounds of traffic. The old road *did* meet up with the highway. She breathed a sigh of relief.

The brush next to the highway was an impenetrable mass and Lauren had to ride Trooper off the old road and into the ancient forest to get around it. When she broke out of the trees, she looked back. The old road was completely hidden by vegetation.

"We'll come back some other day and explore, Trooper. I promise," she said and patted the gelding on the neck. "And I forgive you for wanting to go the wrong direction. I know you were just having fun too, and didn't want to go home yet. Right?"

Trooper snorted in response and looked longingly toward the hidden road. Then he drew a deep sigh and stepped toward Aunt April's.

Chapter Eleven

After taking off his tack, Lauren put Trooper back in his stall and gave him some grain. Coyote and Orion were outside in the paddock and the barn was quiet. Trooper munched his oats, his skin twitching with pleasure as the body brush swept over his coat. When Lauren finished grooming him, she patted him on the shoulder. "You're a good boy, Troops. I know I'm not a very good rider yet, but I'm learning. Soon you'll know exactly what I want you to do. Lisa thinks I might even be good enough to enter in the beginner classes at the fair."

Trooper turned his head and looked at her with shining eyes. The subdued light in the barn warmed his glossy coat with soft highlights. His mane and tail shimmered in the half light. Lauren hugged him around his neck. "I'll let you have a rest, boy. And then later on when Charity and Kjerstina get home and we've eaten supper, we can go for an evening ride." She loosened her arms around his neck and ran her hand along his side as she retreated toward the door of the stall. As she was fastening the special clip onto his door, Trooper lipped at the hay she had left him, pulling out the choicest, greenest morsels, and watched her with dark eyes.

Aunt April had just started making supper. "Can I help?" asked Lauren.

"Of course, Dear," replied Aunt April. "You can peel the potatoes. The peeler is in the drawer to my right." She motioned toward the drawer with her elbow, her hands busy fashioning hamburger patties.

Lauren grabbed the peeler and picked up the first potato.

"How do you like it here, so far, Lauren?" Aunt April asked.

"I love it. Trooper is the most awesome horse," she said, then added quickly, "And you guys are great too."

Aunt April laughed. "But it's Trooper who steals the show. I don't blame you. I loved the horse I had as a girl with all my heart."

"You had a horse? What was he like?"

"He was a she, actually. Her name was Comanche and she was the most beautiful horse in the world, at least to me. She was a pinto, a bay and white tobiano pinto, to be precise."

"What's tobiano?"

"It just means she was white with brown spots, instead of brown with white spots. The one with white spots is called an overo."

"Weird."

"Anyway, she was the fastest horse in the neighborhood. She was never beaten in a race. Not once. And she was the best barrel racer I ever owned."

"You used to be a barrel racer, Aunt April? Wow!"

The ring of the phone interrupted their conversation.

"Can you get that Lauren?" her Aunt asked. "My hands are all sticky."

"Sure." She picked up the receiver. "Hello?"

"Hey, Kiddo. How're you doing?"

"Hi, Dad, I'm doing great," answered Lauren. "Do you have time to talk today or do you have to rush off."

He chuckled. "I have time. And I'm sorry I've been gone so much. I'll explain everything when I see you. I have good news for you."

"Yeah?" prompted Lauren.

"I'm coming out to see you right away. I'll be leaving in the morning."

"That's awesome, Dad! I can show you Trooper then. Maybe Charity will let you ride Orion and we can go out together. I found a hidden road today that we could explore. It's so cool. Oh, Dad, are you bringing Sweetie? She'd love it."

Lauren's dad was laughing. "I don't know when I've heard anyone so excited to see me. You always do my heart good. And of course, I'll bring Sweetie. I'll be driving out, so she can ride in back. I hope she doesn't get carsick this time."

"Me too," said Lauren. "Hey, why are you coming out now anyway? What about your job? What about the stalker?"

"I'm taking some time off work. I couldn't stand being away from my favorite girl any longer," he said, ignoring her second question.

"But what about the stalker?" Lauren persisted.

"We can talk about that when I get there, okay?"

"So you've found something out," concluded Lauren. "Is that why you're coming out early?"

Her dad laughed again. "You are persistent, aren't you? Yes, the mystery is solved, but I'd rather tell you about it face-to-face, okay? Do you think you can wait until tomorrow evening? I should get there about six."

Lauren grimaced. "I guess I can wait," she said slowly. "But it'll be hard. Why can't you tell me now?"

"It'll take too much time to explain and besides, this way you'll have more time to get Trooper all fancied up."

"Yeah. Hey, you should have seen him today, Dad. He looked awesome." Lauren went on to tell him about the visit to the tack store and her purchases. She tried to describe how beautiful Trooper was, but knew her words didn't do him justice. "You'll just have to see him, Dad," she finally concluded.

"I'll bring my camera too," he offered. "Now how about you let me talk to your Aunt April for a minute, Kiddo. I have to let her know to expect us."

"Us?"

"Uh, Sweetie and me."

"Okay, Dad. I can't wait to see you. Bye."

Lauren held the receiver while Aunt April washed her hands and dried them. When she took the phone and started talking, Lauren went back to peeling potatoes.

Aunt April took the receiver from her ear. "Lauren?" she asked. "Would you mind running out to the cellar and getting me a couple jars of peaches for dessert?"

"Sure," said Lauren. She walked out the back door and slipped on her shoes that she'd left on the porch. The cellar was the old fashioned kind, built into a hillside near the house.

"Okay, Alan. She's gone," she heard Aunt April's voice come from the kitchen. The door was still open a crack and Aunt April's voice was clear. Knowing she probably shouldn't, Lauren moved a little closer to the opening.

"What?" Aunt April's voice was shocked. "It *is* her then."

The stalker, thought Lauren. *I shouldn't be listening. I should wait until Dad tells me himself.* Slowly she backed away from the door, trying not to make the boards squeak.

"Did Beth explain herself? About where she's been all these years?"

For a moment, Lauren couldn't move. Couldn't breath. *Beth. The person in the blue car was named Beth. Was it a coincidence? A horrible, terrible coincidence?* She tried to move her feet from where they were rooted to the porch.

"I thought we'd never see her again." Aunt April's voice floated from the crack in the door. "Poor Lauren. She thinks…"

And Lauren ran, her thoughts tearing through her head like a herd of wild, crazed horses. *The stalker is my mom! She wasn't killed in that car accident. This is even worse than her being dead. She left us because she wanted to! She abandoned us!*

Somehow, Lauren found herself in the barn. Trooper threw his head into the air, startled, when she rocketed into his stall, his halter in her hands. Within seconds, the halter was on his head. She led him from the barn and ran to the gate. She undid the special latch and flung it into the grass. Lauren barely had the presence of mind to close the gate behind her. Then she led Trooper to the wood-shed, to the chopping block. She jumped from the block onto his back, and dug her heels into his side. As she trotted Trooper down the driveway, she heard the back door bang open and Aunt April call to her to wait.

Automatically, Lauren pulled back on the lead rope. But then she leaned forward and her heels dug into Trooper's side. *I can't talk to her! I can't talk to anyone about this. Not now. I need to think. How could my mom*

77

betray me like this? And does Dad just think I'll accept her back, after she walked out? Is that what he really meant by 'us'? That not just he and Sweetie are coming to Misty Lake? Is he bringing her here to try to make up with me?

Lauren's hands shook with disbelief and anger as she gripped Trooper's mane. When they reached the road, she urged him into a gallop. She had to get away. Far, far away. When Trooper reached the hidden road they had explored that day, he turned into the forest. Lauren didn't even try to stop him. It was the perfect place to go. Charity and Kjerstina would find her if she went to the spring or down any of the other trails they had ridden together.

After they were on the old road, Lauren pulled Trooper to a walk. No one would find her now. The gelding wove easily through the bushes and saplings on the road and Lauren became lost in her thoughts. Why would a mother leave her daughter? Her family? Lauren thought of the last time she had seen her, laughing and telling them not to fuss over her so much in the hospital. Then her mind turned to the time her dad told Lauren her mother was dead.

He must have known she wasn't. He was lying to me, she realized and for the first time, tears prickled her eyes. *Why did he tell me she was dead? Did he do something to make her leave? But he only ever took care of her, just like he does with me. They were always laughing. They were happy. Weren't they? He should have told me the truth about her!*

When Trooper came to an abrupt stop, Lauren jerked out of her thoughts. She watched, dazed, as he bumped an old wooden gate on the road with his nose. The gate fell

with a crash and Trooper picked his way over it. Lauren was just about to pull him to a stop, when they rounded a corner.

A dilapidated house stood in front of them. It looked like an old farmhouse. A run-down barn leaned precariously on the other side of the overgrown yard. Abandoned, just like her. There was no sound in the stable yard, no movement. Not even the flutter of leaves or a breath of wind. Not the smallest peep of a bird.

"Where are we, Trooper?" Lauren whispered as if afraid to stir something inside the old house or barn. "Where on earth have you brought me?"

Chapter Twelve

Trooper tossed his head and tried to step forward into the weed-choked yard. "Whoa," said Lauren and held him back. She shivered in spite of the warmth of the early evening.

The sides of the house were so weathered they were almost black and the windows were dark with grime. Some of the glass was broken. Lauren couldn't have imagined a place more spooky and decrepit if she'd tried. Her eyes explored the barn across the yard. There was something even creepier about the barn, something indefinable. It was dark like the house, but it seemed scarier, especially in the unnatural stillness. Lauren listened again for a noise – any noise, but there was nothing. When Trooper took another step forward, she pulled him back again. He whinnied softly to her and turned his head.

"What is it, Trooper?" she asked. "Why did you want to come here so much?"

Trooper whinnied again and stepped forward. This time Lauren let him walk toward the barn. He wove through the saplings and brush to stand in front of the double doors. Lauren reined him to a stop and looked up at the huge building. A black opening yawned above her. "That must be a hay loft," she said in a voice still shaking with emotion. "It's an old farm. I wonder what happened to the people who lived here. Why they left?"

She looked behind her at the house. She could use the porch to stand on when she wanted to jump onto Trooper's back. She slipped off the horse, then reached to touch his warm side, drawing comfort from his solid presence. The barn door was barred. Lauren was surprised, when she pulled up on the board attached to the door on her left, that it lifted so easily from the bracket on the right. She pulled the left door back until it hit a small tree. Trooper took a step forward and pushed his head through the door, but Lauren pulled him back.

"You just wait here, buddy," she said. "I'm going to explore a bit." She tied him to the tree and turned back to the opening. As she passed through, she pushed the right side of the double door open. It too, only opened a few feet before hitting a thick wild rose bush. But it was enough to let the light in. Late sunshine spilled across the dusty board floor.

The barn was huge. Ten stalls lined the back wall and all the stall doors were firmly closed except one. To Lauren's right, at the end of the building, she could see a chicken coop and to her left was a large pen with a high wire fence.

Lauren walked to the right first, looking around her as she went. Pieces of farm machinery rusted against the wall opposite the stalls. She thought it was strange that they were parked so neatly and spaced so evenly along the wall.

Someone must have loved this place, she thought. *It looks like they took good care of it before they left. I wonder why they didn't sell their stuff before they went? I bet it was worth a lot of money back then.*

Lauren came to the chicken coop at the end of the barn

and pulled the door open. The rusty hinges protested loudly in the stillness and dust flew from the bottom of the door as it scraped across the barn floor.

It was dark inside the chicken coop. All the windows to the outside were shuttered. Lauren picked her way to the first window, unlatched it and pulled the shutters open. Light and fresh air billowed through the wire covering the window and Lauren looked around the abandoned enclosure. *There's just a whole bunch of dust and feathers in here*, she thought. *Wait, what's this?*

She scuffed a pile of feathers with her foot and felt something solid. She jumped back against the wall, bumping one of the shutters with her shoulder. It banged shut, darkening the chicken coop even more.

It's a dead chicken, Lauren realized. She put her hand over her mouth and stared into the shadows. *All those feathery lumps are dead chickens! There must be twenty or thirty. Or more.*

"Oh God," Lauren whispered and leaped between the piles of feathers and out the door. She slammed it behind her.

Were they sick? she wondered. *The poor, poor things.* Her next thought made her cringe. *What if there are more dead animals in the barn?* A prickle of revulsion crawled up her spine.

Fearing the worst, Lauren walked toward the closest stall, the one with the open door. To her relief, it was empty. But inside the second stall lay the bones of a large animal. They were picked clean and tumbled in disarray over the dirty yellow straw. Lauren covered her mouth again and hurried along the row of stalls. All the other stalls were filled with the bones of dead animals. The skeleton in the last stall looked a bit different than the others. When Lauren noticed the iron shoes on the hooves, she realized it was a horse.

So the others are cows, thought Lauren and felt suddenly nauseous. Almost against her will, she glanced inside the large pen before she left the barn. A number of smaller skeletons were scattered behind the high wire. Then she was outside and her arms were around Trooper's neck.

What happened to them? The thought screamed through her head. *It's impossible for so many different kinds of animals to get sick at the same time and die. And if they had, the farmer would have taken care of their bodies. No, they were abandoned, the poor things! And they died of thirst and starvation. They died of neglect, locked inside tiny wooden stalls. How could anyone do that, just leave all their animals to die? As if animals can't hurt or feel terrified!*

Sudden rustling came from above her. With a gasp, Lauren froze. Slowly, she pulled away from Trooper and looked at the opening to the loft. Visions of bears and cougars leaping out at her raced through her mind, even though she knew the thought of a bear jumping out was silly. With shaky fingers, Lauren fumbled with Trooper's lead rope, her eyes locked on the loft opening. She stopped when a tiny orange and white head peeked over the edge of the loft. The kitten stared at her for a moment as if trying to figure out what she was, then disappeared.

"Here, kitty," Lauren called. The little head reappeared, this time with a tabby companion. Lauren was surprised at how enormous their ears were in comparison to their thin faces.

"You're so cute, even if you do look like big-eared bats," Lauren crooned. "Come here, kitties." Two sets of large eyes looked at her suspiciously. When she took a step toward the barn, the kittens darted away. Lauren could hear the straw rustling, then scratching on the inside wall of the barn.

There must be a way to get up and down from the loft on the inside, she realized and hurried to the door. She looked inside just in time to see the two kittens jump from a decaying ladder that stretched up the wall beside a rusty tractor. It led to a hole in the ceiling, the inside entrance to the loft.

Lauren watched the kittens race toward the chicken coop end of the barn, then disappear through a tiny hole in the wall. She ran outside to stand beside Trooper again. The kittens were leaping through the undergrowth. She could hear their rustling and see glimpses of them as they raced toward the house. A few seconds later, they bounded up the steps to the house. Halfway across the porch, the orange kitten leaped on top of his companion and the two rolled into a tumbled heap. Lauren laughed at their antics and the two kittens stopped to look at her. Now that Lauren could see their whole bodies, she was shocked.

They're terribly thin, she thought. *No wonder their ears seem big. The rest of their bodies are so skinny. I wonder what happened to their mother?*

"Here, kitties," she called again. "Come and I'll take you home and feed you." The orange kitten was curious and took a step toward her, but the tabby was more timid. He scooted in through the open door.

They're wild, Lauren realized, *and something's happened to their mother. Without her, they can't find enough to eat.* "I wonder how they got way out here," she said, turning back to Trooper.

She led the gelding to the front porch of the house and

85

tied him to one of the support beams with a triple knot so he couldn't untie himself. Then she turned her attention to the house. Carefully she walked up the steps and across the porch. The boards were weak and she tested each one before she put her entire weight on it, then she pushed the door the rest of the way open and stepped inside.

Lauren found herself in an old kitchen. It had been cheerful at one time, but now the curtains had faded to gray and the floor was brown with dirt and debris. Dusty dishes and mouse droppings were scattered across the countertop. A rusty, old-fashioned fridge and stove stood against opposite walls and one window was broken. Broken glass, twigs, and dried leaves were scattered across the table. A squirrel or some other small creature had made a nest on top of the fridge, but the animal was gone and the pile of sticks and moss looked as forlorn and abandoned as the rest of the house. Lauren glanced around but didn't see the kittens.

She walked across the kitchen and into a living room. This room was in even worse repair. Over the years, countless woodland creatures had stolen stuffing from the couches and chairs for nests and burrows. Holes were pecked, chewed, and ripped in the rotten fabric and rain had swept in from another broken window. The floorboards around the window were warped and cracked from the rain spilling across the floor. Lauren stopped to listen, but there was nothing to hear. She pulled the couches away from the wall and looked behind them, but there was no sign of the kittens.

They could be inside one of the couches, she realized. *There are so many holes.* She considered ripping into the old couches, but then changed her mind. *I'll check the rest of the rooms first*, she decided.

86

Lauren walked through a doorway leading from the living room into a tiny dark hallway. Two of the three doors in the hallway stood open and Lauren peeked into the first one. It was a bathroom. She stepped inside and looked into the grimy bathtub, then behind the door. There was no other place for the kittens to hide and when she didn't see them, Lauren moved on to the next room, closing the bathroom door behind her.

The second room held a double bed and a fancy dresser. *Now this looks more interesting,* Lauren thought as she walked to the dresser. She picked up a picture sitting on the dresser. A man, a woman, and a girl who looked about nine years old gazed back at her. A family. They were smiling at each other and looked happy. Quickly, Lauren put the picture back, facedown.

Lauren picked up a small perfume bottle from the dresser and sprayed some on her wrists, then sniffed. "Ew gross," she said and put the bottle back on the dresser. "I smell like rotten flowers." She rubbed her wrists on the bedspread in an effort to get off some of the scent. When she sniffed again, she wrinkled her nose in disgust. *Now I smell like rotten flowers, mildew and dirty laundry. Ew!*

Lauren slid open the top dresser drawer. Clothes had been chewed into mouse nests. She poked at the threads and jumbles of disintegrating cloth, then shut the drawer and opened the one beneath it. There in a soft bundle of chewed paper was a little wiggle of pink. With her fingertip, Lauren carefully pushed back some of the paper fluffs. Four tiny pink mice squirmed in the nest as the cooler air brushed over their hairless, fragile bodies.

"Sorry, little guys," Lauren said and gently pulled the fluff back over them. A woman's face looked up at her from the pile of fluff, part of a chewed up photo. "It looks like you made good use of that old photo album, anyway." Slowly, she pushed the drawer back in. She dropped to her knees in front of the bed and peered into the shadows beneath. No kittens.

But they have to be here somewhere. This is the last room they can get inside, unless they squeezed underneath that closed door. They're awfully skinny, she reasoned as she climbed to her feet and walked into the hallway. *Or they may have another way into the room.* She walked to the closed door, turned the knob and pushed it open.

Wow, what a cool room, she thought as she stepped inside. The bedroom was much better preserved than the rest of the house. The window was still intact and the door being shut had given it some protection against the woodland creatures and weather.

Lauren turned a full circle in the center of the room. It was obvious that the person who had lived here was artistic. Paintings covered the walls. Some were of plants and flowers, some of mountains and meadows, and some were of animals. Lauren looked closely at a painting of a bay mare with a buckskin foal. "Cool. He's the same color as Trooper," she said and touched the foal in the painting. "He even has Trooper's crescent shaped star on his forehead."

Books lay in a stack on the night table and some of Lauren's favorites were in the pile. She picked up the top book, a copy of Black Beauty, and leafed through it. The line drawings were colored in with pencil crayons. Ginger was a bright red chestnut with a blaze and Black Beauty glowed a velvet black with blue highlights to make him look shiny.

Lauren looked around at the pictures again. *I'll use my*

paintings at home to decorate my room. I've always just hidden them away in my bottom drawer, but they're as good as these ones and these look so cool inside the frames. And my mom was an artist. A rush of warmth swept over Lauren's face. *Is an artist. She didn't die. She just abandoned me.*

Lauren slumped down on the bed and put her face in her hands. A small cloud of dust rose from the bedspread. How could she have forgotten? Lauren felt tears prick at her eyes and immediately straightened.

No! I'm not going to cry, she vowed. *I'm never going to cry about her again. She doesn't deserve it!*

Her hand brushed against a piece of paper lying on the bedspread. She looked down. It was a photograph, ripped into little pieces. A chill touched the back of Lauren's neck. She pushed the pieces around to see if she could put them together. *It's a man,* she realized. *Why would someone rip up his picture?*

"But I would've ripped up my Dad's picture just an hour ago," she whispered. She pushed the last pieces of the photo in place. The man's eyes were sad, his mouth a tense line across his face.

Just like my dad's will be when he finds out I ran away. She sighed. *I think I know why he didn't tell me the truth about Mom. As usual, he was trying to protect me. He wanted me to think she had no choice when she left us. He did what he thought was right for me, even though it wasn't. He should have told me the truth. But I can forgive him. It's her I'll never forgive. Never. No matter what!*

89

Chapter Thirteen

Lauren raised her head to look out the window. The shadows stretched longer across the yard. *It's getting late*, she realized. *I better hurry. I don't want to be stuck here when it gets dark. Those kittens have got to be here somewhere.*

A sudden scrambling noise came from the front of the house. "Gotcha," whispered Lauren. She moved quickly and quietly out of the room and along the hall, then peeked around the corner but the living room was empty. As quietly as she could, she crept toward the kitchen and leaned through the doorway.

Lauren smiled as the orange and white kitten skittered across the floor with the tabby in close pursuit. They were playing. The tabby jumped on his brother's head and bit his ear. Lauren held her breath as the two kittens rolled around in mock battle in the middle of the kitchen. The orange kitten was slightly bigger than the tabby, who meowed as his tail was attacked. He reached out and whacked the orange kitten on the nose, then ran toward the corner of the room and disappeared through a door.

Lauren hadn't noticed the door when she first walked through the kitchen. It was painted the same color as the walls and was only slightly ajar. The orange kitten saw

Lauren's movement as she turned her head. He froze on the spot, his eyes huge in the unlit kitchen, then gave a tiny mew and scampered toward the door and disappeared after his littermate.

Lauren walked across the room and swung the door open. Stairs led down to a cellar. It wasn't as dark in the cellar as Lauren expected and carefully she stepped onto the top step.

"Kitty, kitty," she called. "Come here." She could see the orange kitten sitting halfway down the stairs and the tabby looking at her from between two storage shelves. "I won't hurt you, Spunky," she said in a soothing voice to the orange kitten. "Or you either, uh...Tiger." She glanced at where the tabby had been sitting, but he was gone. "I'm going to take you to a nice home where you can have lots to eat. I promise."

She took a cautious step down. The stairs didn't look too safe. Spunky darted down the rest of the stairs and ran to join his brother. Lauren shut the kitchen door behind her, then quickly descended the rest of the way. The cellar was dim but she could still see. Most of the shelves were empty and the light from one high window flowed through the unblocked shelves. The kitten huddled on the floor and watched her with terrified eyes.

They know they're trapped, thought Lauren. *I've got to tame them without scaring them any more. If only I had something to feed them.* She looked around the cellar. Canned goods. Glass home-canned jars lined one of the shelves.

Moving slowly so she wouldn't frighten the kittens, Lauren walked to the jars. Most of them were fruit and pickles. But two of the jars were filled with something brown. Lauren took one of the jars off the shelf and rubbed the dirty glass. *This looks like meat.* She rubbed the top of the jar in case anything was written there. The words, "Moose Meat" appeared as she wiped away the grime.

Gross. But the kittens won't mind. It'll be a feast to them. Lauren tried to unscrew the lid, but it wouldn't budge. She put the jar between her knees and squeezed, then gripped the lid with both hands and tried to turn it. That didn't work either.

"Don't worry, kitties," she said looking up at the kittens. Curiosity was getting the best of their fear. Spunky was inching toward her, Tiger right behind him. Lauren gently banged the edge of the lid against the wooden shelf, then tried to turn it again. When it didn't open, she banged it again, a little harder.

This time the jar lid turned. Lauren pulled off the outer ring and pried off the sealed lid. She was glad to hear a faint sucking noise when she loosened the lid. That meant the jar was still airtight and the meat was safe to eat. "The last thing I want to do is poison you guys," she said as she sat down, the open jar beside her. She dipped her fingers into the juice floating around the chunks of meat and held her hand out to the kittens. They didn't hesitate. Both Spunky and Tiger rushed forward and their tiny pink tongues had licked up the juice within a second.

"Just a minute, guys," said Lauren. She pulled a chunk of moose meat out of the jar and broke it in two, then laid it on the floor in front of her crossed legs. The kittens started to gulp down the food, growling at each other and her as they ate. Lauren gave them another piece and they ate more slowly. The growling faded away. After their third piece each, Lauren reached out with her hand again. Spunky started to lick her fingers even though he still had meat in front of him. Then he started to purr. Tiger joined right in, his purr seeming far too large for his tiny body. Lauren stroked the kittens' knobby backs and soon they were in her lap, Tiger curled into a rumbling ball as Spunky washed his face with his paw.

"Time to go home," said Lauren. Gently she scooped them into her arms and stood. The kittens didn't even struggle. "Poor babies," she murmured. "You're just glad to have someone take care of you, aren't you? I wonder what happened to your mother?" Careful not to jostle them too much, she climbed the stairs. "Now I just need something to put you in so I can take you home. I wonder if there's something in the house I can use. Or the barn." She wrinkled her nose. She really didn't want to go back into the barn.

But there is something I can use there, she remembered. *That leather feedbag hanging outside the dead horse's stall.* The feedbag was the kind farmers used to use to feed their horses grain from during a break in the field work. They would buckle the halter part over the horse's head and the bag part, full of grain, would fit over its nose. It was perfect for transporting the kittens.

Lauren's forehead beaded with sweat. She would have to go back into the barn. When she stepped outside the house, she was surprised it was even warmer than inside the house. And everything seemed more still than before. She stepped off the porch, the kittens in her arms, and looked up at the sky.

"Oh my." It sounded like something Aunt April would say. Lauren didn't think she'd ever said "oh my" in her life. But she didn't know what else to say. Ominous clouds swirled in the sky. *No wonder its dark so early,* she thought. *But that doesn't explain why it's so hot. Why it's so still. There's not a breath of movement. No breeze. No nothing.*

The kittens wiggled in her arms and Spunky tried to jump down. A worried expression sat on his face. And Lauren understood. It was the calm, the unnatural calm that happens before the worst storms. And this promised to be one giant of a storm.

"It's okay, Spunky," she said and hurried past Trooper toward the barn. "We'll be on our way soon, Troops. I've just got to get that bag, then we'll go."

She was halfway across the yard when the wind hit them. Lauren clutched the kittens to her chest, but she was too late. Like small slippery eels, they slid from her fingers and leaped toward the barn. Lauren was right behind them. She was just steps from the building when the skies opened and water poured out. She was soaked before she could slip in through the barn door. She glanced back to see Trooper through the downpour, his back hunched against the rain, his ears pinned back.

"Hang on, Trooper!" she called. "I'll be right back!" Thunder boomed around them, swallowing Lauren's words. The wind moaned against the barn and pummelled the blackened boards with rumbling waves of rain. Lauren could hardly see Trooper through the curtain of water that streamed from the roof. She ran to the stall and grabbed the feedbag, then looked around for the kittens. The barn was cast in shadow, the kittens nowhere to be seen.

"Kitties?"

A tiny mew. Lauren spun around to see Tiger walking out of the empty stall, his tail in the air. She hurried forward and bent to pick him up. And then the barn door slammed shut.

Absolute total darkness.

Lauren screamed and jumped back, the kitten forgotten.

Keep calm, keep calm! Don't be a wimp!

Her breath came shallow and quick as her eyes shifted in the dark, trying to see anything. Anything at all.

Sudden unbidden images of the animal bones shot into her mind. They were shifting in their dirty straw. Coming together. Rebuilding themselves into the creatures they had once been. They would be coming for her! She had to run. Hide. She had to get away!

There's nowhere to run, the reasonable part of her mind interjected. *No one to hear me scream. Be sensible! Don't panic!*

But it was too late. She stumbled in the direction of the door, her outstretched hands desperately reaching for the rough wood. There was a faint glimmer of light to her left and she inched toward it. It was the crack between the two doors.

Lauren pushed the door. Nothing! She threw her entire weight against it, not caring if it sprung open and she fell into the pounding rain. She had to escape! The door rattled and gave an inch or two, then bounced back. She could imagine the bony horse standing behind her, reaching out to touch her.

Don't be stupid, don't be stupid, she repeated to herself over and over, and threw herself against the door again. *Why isn't it opening? Why can't I get out?*

In a moment of rational thought, she wondered if she had the right spot, if she was actually pushing on the door or if she was to the side of it. She reached out along the wood, terrified she was going to touch bone. The hinges were there. It had to be the door. But why wouldn't it open?

The answer came in a flash. The bar had fallen across the door. On the outside.

As she stood there, logical awareness of her situation trickled into her mind. Night was coming on. No one knew where she was. Trooper was tied with a triple knot he could never undo and couldn't go for help. And she was trapped.

No, not just trapped, revised Lauren. *I'm trapped in a decaying barn full of dead animals. I've got to get out of here. Before I go insane!*

Chapter Fourteen

Something touched Lauren's leg. She leaped into the air without thinking. When she came down, her ankle turned and she sprawled across the hard wooden floor. Desperately, she crawled away from whatever had touched her. She could hear something scratching the barn floor as it scrambled the opposite direction and then Tiger's worried mew as he greeted Spunky.

Lauren had never been so happy to hear a cat meow, to hear another living creature. Breathing heavily, she climbed to her feet. "Sorry guys," she said, her voice trembling. "I didn't know it was you. You can come see me now. Are you scared? I am."

She put her hand out to find the barn wall, then slid to the floor. "Come on, kitties," she called in her most coaxing voice. A tiny mew halfway across the barn, then a few seconds later, a damp nose touched her fingers. Lauren reached out in the dark and pulled the kitten into her lap. She could feel the second one climb in after his brother. "Sorry to scare you guys. I should have known better. It never does any good to panic. I'm just glad you two are forgiving."

She looked around the barn. Her eyes were adjusting to the darkness. She could make out the faint hulking shapes of the farm machinery beside her, the stall doors in front of her. And most important, no skeletons. A shiver jagged down her back. "I've got to get out of here before it gets dark," she whispered, more to herself than to the kittens. The rain thundering on the roof drowned out her words. "I've got to get back to Aunt April's."

Carefully, she lifted the kittens, one after the other, from her lap. "Now stay put, you two," she said, though she knew they wouldn't understand. "I don't want to step on you. Or have you scare me again." With a sudden thought, she pulled off her light jacket. She put in on the floor, then feeling for the kittens in the dark, she put them on the jacket. She petted them until they settled down again. "If anything touches me while I explore, I want to be sure it's something to be scared of," she joked. When Spunky mewed, she smiled into the darkness. "I know. I'm being dumb. But that's better than being scared out of my mind." She gave them each one last stroke, then straightened.

Okay, now I need to think. There has to be a way out. Her mind did a quick mental inventory. There were the double doors she had come through and the windows in the chicken coop. And there could be other possibilities. *Maybe windows in the large pen to the left of the double doors,* she thought. *Or in some of the stalls. I might not have noticed. The bones were so horrible that I was only looking at them.* The thought of stepping over and among the bones in the dark while searching for an escape route, made her heart pound faster and her breath quicken. *I'll try that only if all the other plans fail,* she decided.

First, she went to the double doors. She pushed on them again and the bar rattled against the doors. But it stayed firmly in place. Lauren could see it through the

99

crack between the two panels. It wasn't as dark outside and the rain was already slowing down. The clouds were moving on, leaving the rundown house and barn to a normal twilight. She still couldn't see Trooper across the yard. It was too dark for that. But when she called to him, he answered her, his neigh loud enough to be heard above the pounding rain.

"I'll be out soon, Troops," called Lauren. "Don't worry. I'll just be a few minutes, okay?" Trooper nickered in response and Lauren went back to her investigation. The crack between the two doors was too narrow to squeeze her fingers through; far too narrow for a board or something else that could push the bar up.

But the people who lived here must have had some way to open it, she reasoned. There must be a handle or rope or something. In her search, her fingers discovered a small hole about the size of her thumb, about an arm's length above the bar.

That's it, she realized. *They had a rope going through here with the other end tied to the bar. That's what opened it from the inside. But the rope's rotted away.* She turned in frustration.

"On to the chicken coop," she said to the kittens in a falsely cheerful voice as she passed. There was no response. Lauren hoped they were still sleeping and not wandering about the barn where she would step on them. She felt along the line of machinery toward the chicken coop door. The door still hung open, just as she had left it earlier when she had run from the coop, horrified to find so many dead chickens. She crept into the darkness. The shutters on the first window were still open, allowing the evening to lend a faint light that spread across the floor. Across the bones that lay scattered there. Lauren picked her way around them the best she could, hating the crunch that came from beneath her feet whenever she inadvertently stepped on one. Her skin crawled with revulsion.

Finally she reached the window. She pulled the shutters all the way back, curled her fingers through the holes in the wire and tugged. The wire hardly moved. Lauren jerked backward with all her strength.

"Ow!" she cried and pulled her hands away. The wire had cut into her fingers, but had barely budged. She tried the next window and the next, but they were all the same. Strong. Unmoveable. There could be no escape from the chicken coop.

Lauren crept to the chicken coop door and looked out at the darkness that spread before her. *What next?* she wondered. *The stalls? Or the other big pen?* Both seemed incredibly unappealing. *But I've got to do one or the other quick. It's going to be pitch black in here soon. And then I won't be able to see anything.*

Lauren moved along the line of stalls, her eyes trying to pierce through the shadows to see if any windows were against the back wall. But none of the stalls had a square of lightness at the back of it. When she reached the last stall, she heard one of kittens meow.

"What's wrong, buddy. Where are you?"

The kitten's mew came again and Lauren made her way to where she thought her jacket lay. When she drew near, she dropped to her knees and felt the floor in front of her with outstretched hands. After a minute, she felt its wet softness. The kittens were gone.

"Where are you, guys?" she called again. A mew came from above her head. *What?* thought Lauren, momentarily confused. Then she remembered. The loft! The kittens were back in the loft.

And there's a huge open door to the outside in the loft, remembered Lauren, excitement making her heart race. *I know I could find a way down. There's got to be some ropes or boards or something up there I can use. As a last resort, I can jump. It's high, but not that high. And it's a lot better than spending the night in this horrible barn.*

As fast as she could, she moved to where she remembered the ladder to the loft being. Within seconds, she felt the rungs beneath her hands. She lifted her foot and put it on the first rung, then pulled herself up. The ladder creaked beneath her, but it held. She reached higher with her foot and hand and pulled herself up another rung. "I'm coming, kitties," she said when she heard the curious mew come from above her.

When she was halfway up, one of the rungs came loose. Lauren's feet fell back to the rung below it and her she gripped the ladder tightly with her hands. She looked down. The barn below was pitch black now. She could see nothing but darkness. In her imagination, the animal bones began to stir in their stalls again. Started to reassemble themselves. Started to move toward her.

Don't be silly! she commanded herself. With a desperate lunge she moved her foot up two rungs and pushed upward. Her hands clutched at a higher rung. She could see the sky now, through the trapdoor in the ceiling, and the big opening to the outside. The clouds were almost gone and the fading red of sunset streaked across the sky. Water dripped from the roof of the barn. The two kittens looked down at her, curiously. She was almost there. Just two more rungs. And she could even see the rungs now. She didn't just have to feel for them.

She went up one more rung and felt the ladder shudder. A metallic squeak split the air and Lauren felt the ladder move. The squeak came again and the ladder fell back a little farther. Lauren turned horrified eyes to where it was attached to the barn wall. Her weight was pulling the nails that held it in place right out of the weak, rotting wood. She had to hurry!

A long shriek sliced through the air and the ladder tilted back farther and farther. Without thinking, Lauren pushed upward and made a wild grab for the edge of the loft. But she was too late. The ladder came free with a final wrenching sound and fell backward. There was nothing she could do.

Lauren sprawled across the barn floor, gasping for air with the ladder on top of her. She cried out in pain where the jagged wood had stabbed into her arm and raked across her back. She struggled for a moment, wild and unthinking, the ladder crushing her into the floor. Then stars exploded in front of her eyes and she slipped into darkness.

Chapter Fifteen

Lauren wasn't sure how much time had passed when she first noticed the light behind her eyes. But she couldn't open them to see. Her body wasn't working. Then the light disappeared.

When she became conscious again, she heard murmurs. Far away conversation. *They've come to rescue me.* The single thought made its way through the fog in her mind. Then there was silence.

Darkness again.

An animal sniffed at her. Growled. *A dog,* she thought, but she couldn't see it. Still couldn't open her eyes.

Dark again.

"But I don't want to go," Lauren heard herself say. Her eyes were shut, but she could tell she was crying. Her tears were choking her words. "Daddy, please," she begged.

"You have to," said her dad. Lauren could imagine him shaking his head, even though she couldn't see him. "It's for the best," he continued. "I know you don't see why it's important now, but someday you will."

"No, I won't. I belong here. I belong where you are. Where mom used to live," said Lauren's voice. Somewhere in her mind, Lauren thought it was strange she couldn't feel her lips moving. "She wouldn't want you to send me away. If she were alive, she'd stop you," she concluded.

He sighed. "I'll come to visit you and you can come home every Christmas and summer holidays. It won't be that bad. I promise. Now go gather the eggs while I finish milking Bessie. Then we can have breakfast."

Breakfast? But it's past suppertime. And gather the eggs? Lauren wondered. *I've never gathered eggs in my life. Dad should know that. Hey! How can my dad be here?* She heard something scrape across the floor, loud in the silence that followed his words.

"I'm not hungry," she whispered.

"Mrs. Carter is going to be here in a few hours to pick you up and you've got a long drive ahead of you. You're going to get hungry, Lizzie," warned her dad.

Lauren became even more puzzled. *Who was Mrs. Carter? And who was Lizzie?* She tried to open her mouth to ask him what he meant, but her mouth wouldn't move. She could hear her voice speaking. "I can't eat. It makes me sick to think about it."

But I didn't say that, Lauren finally realized. *Someone else is here.* She tried to move her head, then her shoulders, but nothing happened. She tried to move her hands to motion to her dad that she couldn't speak, but her hands wouldn't move either. She was paralyzed.

Lauren's heart beat faster and thudding filled her ears. Then somewhere behind the thunder of her heart, Lauren heard someone say, "Please, Daddy. Please let me stay. You've got to let me stay. Mom wouldn't send me away. And you can't either. You just can't."

With all her effort, Lauren opened her eyes a tiny slit. She was lying on a wooden floor. "Where am I?" she whispered. The floor in front of her moved like a pond

105

someone had dropped a stone into. She closed her eyes and drew a shuddering breath. "Help," she said, but her voice was the softest whisper.

"I'm not going to change my mind, Lizzie. This is for the best. There are things you don't know and that I can't tell you. Now just gather the eggs and meet me up at the house."

Lauren lay still and waited for the nausea and dizziness to pass. She opened her eyes for a second, saw a blur of movement, and clamped them shut. She heard heavy footfalls leave the barn and the sound of hooves following. *Well, at least my ears are still working,* she thought. She could feel the dizziness slowly fading away. When she opened her eyes a few minutes later, the floor was still. Lauren took a deep breath.

"Help," she called again. She waited for a moment, but there was no response. The voices were gone. *I must have been dreaming,* she thought. *But what a strange dream. It seemed so real.*

Lauren slowly raised her head to look around. Her vision was still blurred. She could tell she was in a barn, that was all. Then the images of the old homestead, the kittens, the storm and the collapsing ladder rushed back into her mind.

Trooper brought me here, she remembered. *I hope he's okay. I've got to find the kittens and go.* She shut her eyes again. As she gathered strength, another thought popped into her head. *Where's the ladder? I thought it landed on top of me.*

Slowly, she pushed herself to a sitting position and shook her head. The fog was clearing. She could see a line of stalls in front of her. A buckskin gelding looked back at her, his ears pricked forward as he watched her.

"Trooper?" said Lauren in amazement. "How did you get in here? It is you, isn't it?" Slowly, she climbed to her feet expecting to feel stiff. Sore. But she felt fine. No. Better than fine. Now that the dizziness was gone, she felt light and full of energy.

She walked closer, peering ahead through the dissipating fog. It was him! There was the crescent shaped star on his forehead. "Hey buddy," she whispered and reached for his head. "I don't understand. This is too weird." Her hands froze in midair when she heard a door open almost behind her. She spun around to see a eleven or twelve-year-old girl with long, white-blond hair walk out of the chicken coop, a basket of eggs in her hand. The girl closed the door behind her and trudged toward the main barn door.

"I'll be back in a minute, Ben," she said at the door, throwing a look toward Trooper's stall. Her voice was saturated with sadness. "I'm spending all the rest of my time with you. I don't care about breakfast."

Trooper whinnied at her, and with a flick of her silver-gold hair, she was gone.

"Didn't she see me, Trooper? And who is Ben? Does she think I'm a boy or what?" Puzzlement covered Lauren's face. "Hey," she said and her expression suddenly cleared. "The door's open now. Let's get out of here before she comes back. I'll see if the yard is clear."

Lauren hurried to the barn door. Morning sunlight spilled into the barn and she was careful to stay to the side of it. She didn't want the girl to see her until it was too late for her to stop them. She had to get back to Aunt April's as quick as she could. Her dad was going to be there that day. *And my Mom,* remembered Lauren and felt the anger instantly rise up inside her again. She forced it down with an effort. *I'll deal with that when I see her,* she decided and peered around the edge of the open door.

Lauren's mouth dropped open. "What?" she whispered as she looked out into the yard. The bushes and saplings were gone. The yard was covered with dirt and grass – mown grass. The house was in perfect repair and painted white. The blue trim around the windows and doors was cheerful and bright. A red truck stood in front of the house, shiny and clean. She heard a moo coming from her right and looked at a small herd of fawn-colored milk cows grazing near the gate to one of the pastures. In another pasture, one fenced with mesh wire, a herd of goats grazed, their kids jumping and playing in the long grass.

Lauren looked back inside the barn. How had she not noticed? The machinery that had been rusting next to the wall was shiny and well oiled. The ladder stretched up to the loft, strong and firm. There was no dirt or dust. Or bones?

Lauren ran to the nearest stall, her heart pounding faster than her feet hit the floor. When she looked inside she saw clean straw on the floor. A water bucket. Wisps of hay in the manger. But no bones.

Am I dreaming? she wondered and looked wildly at Trooper. *Is all this with Lizzie and her dad a dream? But it's way too real to be a dream. I can even smell cow poo. And I can hear the chickens clucking. And everything looks so real, not dreamlike at all. Trooper is exactly the same. Or is he?*

Slowly Lauren moved closer to the gelding. She stopped outside his stall and her eyes danced over his body. Trooper looked at her patiently, his eyes locked on hers. *Yes, he's the same, but he's different too. What is it?*

Then she knew. *He's younger, he's not even full grown,*

108

she realized and her breath quickened. *And that means it can't be a dream. It means...no! But it must. What else could it be?*

Lauren tried to undo the latch to Trooper's stall so she could go inside. She needed to look at him more closely. Maybe it was just a trick of the light. But the latch beneath her fingers felt strange, as if she was touching it through thick gloves. Lauren glanced down.

With a racing heart, she held her hand up in front of her eyes. Something was wrong. Very wrong. Her hand was colorless. She looked down at the rest of her body and felt heat rise in her face.

I'm like a ghost, she thought with amazement. *All wispy and gray.* She looked around the barn, though she already knew what she would see. *Everything else is in color. It's only me that's not. It's true then. I am a ghost. I've died. But instead of going to heaven, or wherever I'm supposed to go, I've gone back in time. That's why Lizzie didn't see me. That's why I'm faded, like an old photograph. And that's why someone lives here and Trooper is younger. I've died. But why go back in time? It makes no sense.*

Words floated into her mind, her Aunt April's voice. 'He once saved his own life by opening his stall door.'

He was one of the animals abandoned here, Lauren suddenly realized. *He was one of the animals left to die in this barn. Is that why I'm here? To open his stall door and set him free? To save him so he can bring me here years from now?*

And I can die?

Chapter Sixteen

Lauren started when she heard a car drive into the yard outside. Within seconds she was at the door, watching. The shiny black car pulled up to the farmhouse. As soon as the cloud of dust settled, an elegant woman stepped out of the driver's seat.

She looks so out of place, Lauren thought as she watched the woman pick her way past the border collie lying on the top step. The woman acted as if she thought germs were going to leap from the dog to her immaculate skirt. She raised her hand and daintily tapped on the door.

Lizzie is going to hate being at this school, if that's the kind of lady-like stuff they teach, thought Lauren. *I feel even more sorry for her now.*

Lauren watched as the front door opened.

"Welcome, Mrs. Carter," said Lizzie's dad. "Elizabeth is just finishing packing. Would you like a cup of..." The closed door cut off their voices. Lauren was about to pull back from the barn door when she noticed some movement out of the corner of her eye. Lizzie. She was sneaking around the side of the house. She had climbed out a window. Lauren pulled back as Lizzie sprinted across the yard toward her. She raced past Lauren without seeing

111

her, flung Trooper's stall door open and threw her arms around the gold gelding's neck.

She can't see me, Lauren reminded herself. She tried to still her breathing as she crept toward the stall. When she peered over the half door, she saw Lizzie's shoulders shake with silent sobs.

"It's just not fair, Ben," the girl said in a broken voice. "Why did my mom have to die? And now my dad doesn't want me anymore. And I don't know what I did wrong. If I knew I could change, but he won't even tell me. And what am I going to do without you? I won't have anyone in the whole world. I'll be totally alone."

Lauren slipped through the open stall door. Trooper nickered to her and reached out to nuzzle her, but Lizzie didn't look up. She was still sobbing into his mane.

"I understand," Lauren whispered. "My mom died too, or I thought she did. I know how terrible it feels." There was no reaction from Lizzie. *She can't hear me either,* remembered Lauren. Slowly, she reached out and touched Lizzie on the shoulder.

"Leave me alone, Dad. I don't want to go. How can you make me go?" said Lizzie, her voice full of anger. Lauren quickly pulled her hand away and took a step back as Lizzie turned toward her. She looked straight at Lauren, and as Lauren watched, Lizzie's face first became puzzled, then frightened.

"Who's there?" she asked, her eyes searching the barn. Lauren was afraid to move, afraid her feet would rustle the straw and that Lizzie would hear it.

"Mom?" asked Lizzie finally, her voice soft. "Was that you?" She turned back to Trooper and threw her arms around him again. "What if that was my mom?" she said to Trooper. "What if she came to me and I told her to

112

leave me alone? Oh Ben, I mess everything up. Its no wonder Dad doesn't want me anymore." Lizzie slid into the straw at Trooper's feet and buried her face in her hands. She started to sob again.

Without thinking of the consequences, Lauren knelt in the straw beside Lizzie and reached out. She put her hand on the long silver-blond hair and began to stroke it, just as if Lizzie were Spunky or Tiger. Lizzie became quieter. She hugged Trooper's front legs and her sobs slowly died away. Peace floated back into the barn.

Trooper bent his head and sniffed Lauren, then nickered gently. *He's saying thanks,* Lauren realized. *He's thanking me for helping Lizzie.* She put her other hand on his face. "I know how she feels," she whispered to Trooper, knowing that Lizzie couldn't hear her. "All lost and alone. You're the only one who knows I even exist, Trooper."

"Elizabeth," came Lizzie's dad's voice from outside the barn. Lauren felt Lizzie stiffen and pulled her hand away. She caught her breath as Lizzie turned toward her, searching the empty air. One last tear trickled down Lizzie's cheek, but she didn't bother to brush it away. "Thanks Mom," she finally whispered. "Thanks for letting me know I'm not alone, not really. I'll try to be strong. And I love you."

Shakily, she climbed to her feet and threw her arms around Trooper's neck. "Goodbye, Trooper. I'll see you at Christmastime. Don't worry. Dad promised me he wouldn't sell you. You'll always be my best friend."

When Lizzie opened the door to the stall, Lauren slipped out with her. She watched as Lizzie went to the house, kicking at the ground as she walked. Mrs. Carter met her at the door and they shook hands. Lauren was impressed with how straight and strong Lizzie looked as she shook Mrs. Carter's hand. The two of them walked into the house and came out a few minutes later with Lizzie's suitcases.

Her dad put the suitcases in the trunk of the car, then gave Lizzie a hug. Lauren noticed that she didn't hug him back. Her arms hung at her side, her hands curled into fists. She turned away as soon as he released her and climbed into the passenger side of the car.

But she'll be okay, thought Lauren as she watched the car drive away. *She's a survivor. I'm glad I could help her. I wonder if I just changed the past by making Lizzie think her mom was here?*

She walked back to Trooper's stall. The gelding put his head over the door and nickered as she approached. "Will you remember me, Troops? Is that why you brought me here? Or is all this as new to you as it is to me? I really don't understand this time travel stuff." She touched the crescent star between his eyes. He lowered his head further and she laid her cheek against his warmth.

"You know what I think, Troops?" she asked, pulling back to look into his dark brown eyes. She stroked his golden cheek with colorless fingers. "I don't think you brought me here on purpose. I don't think you would hurt me. I think you just remembered this place and wanted to come back."

She paused, deep in thought, her eyes cast down to the barn floor. When she raised them again, her jaw was set, her eyes direct. "I don't think I was sent back in time to save you, Troops. You did that yourself because you're smart and you figured out how to open your stall latch. I don't think I was even sent back to comfort Lizzie, though that might be important too." She shook her head.

114

"No, I'm here to save the animals, all the pretty cows and goats and chickens. And the other horse I haven't even seen yet. And I'm going to do it. Somehow. I promise. But I better hurry. I don't know how much time I have."

Chapter Seventeen

Lauren walked back to the barn door in time to see Lizzie's dad walk into the house, his head hanging down. She almost felt sorry for him when he didn't have the energy to even shut the door behind him. Almost, but not quite.

He's the one who sent her away, she reminded herself. *He doesn't deserve my sympathy. But still, I've got to find out what happens to him. He's the key. It's the only thing I can think of. Something happens to him so he can't take care of the animals. And no one knows anything's wrong, until it's too late to save them.*

Lauren stepped out into the yard. The border collie on the porch was watching her. When it growled, she took a step back. "It's okay, scary dog," she said in her most soothing voice. "I'm not here to hurt anyone. And Sweetie likes me. You would too, if you gave me a chance."

Slowly she walked toward the house, her hand out. When her foot hit the bottom stair leading to the porch, the dog started to bark at her, his hackles raised. "I'm not going to hurt you, pup," she said to the dog, inching closer. "Don't worry. I'm just visiting for a while. As soon as I do what I need to do, I'll go. I promise."

116

Suddenly the door burst open and Lizzie's dad stepped out onto the porch. As he looked across the stable yard, Lauren took the opportunity to race up the rest of the stairs and slip inside the kitchen. "What is it, Jessie?" he asked. The dog stopped barking as soon as Lauren was out of sight. Standing in the kitchen, she could hear him whining, then Lizzie's dad walk toward him. "It's okay, boy," said the man. "I miss her too."

While Lizzie's dad was petting the dog, Lauren hurried through the kitchen and crept up the stairs. She knew what she was looking for. The photo album the mother mouse would one day use to raise her babies in. If Lauren really had gone back into the past, the album would be in fine shape. And she might find a clue there.

She fumbled with the drawer handles and finally was able to slide it open. The album was there, exactly where she thought it would be. Lauren carried it to the bed and sat down with the album on her lap. She paused before opening it. If Lizzie's dad came in what would he see? The album suspected in midair with pages turning? She moved to a chair that sat in the corner. At least here she wouldn't be instantly noticeable if he came into the room.

She turned the pages clumsily, one after the next. The book was full of pictures of first a young girl, then a teenager, and then a young woman. Lauren became more and more intrigued as she leafed through the album. An entire childhood was on display. First, a tiny baby with her mother. Then a six-year-old girl with a golden collie. The girl's head barely reached the dog's shoulder. There she was riding a brown horse when she was twelve. Ribbons fluttering from the horse's bridle.

She looks familiar, thought Lauren and then frowned. *But from where? Maybe she's someone who still lives in*

117

Misty Lake. Someone I've seen in town somewhere, even though she'd be a lot older now.

There was a picture of the same girl with the same horse when she was about sixteen, but this time a black foal stood beside them. *How wonderful,* sighed Lauren. *She had the most perfect life.* There was one photo of the girl with her parents, but Lauren turned that page quickly. "Happy family scenes really aren't my thing right now," she muttered. The last photo in the book showed the young woman in a wedding dress, arm in arm with a young man, her new husband.

Her dress is so beautiful, thought Lauren. *She looks like she loves her husband so much and its obvious he adores her too. He's not the kind of man who would send his daughter away.*

An envelope was tucked between the last page and the back cover. Lauren could tell by feeling it that there were photos inside the envelope. With difficulty, she opened the envelope and photos spilled out onto the photo album pages. Lauren spread them out with awkward fingers. They were photos of the same woman, but she looked different. She was a little older and her face was white and thin. In two of the pictures, she was with the man she had married, but in one his head was turned away from the photographer and in the other he was looking at the ground. Lauren couldn't see his face clearly in either one.

Another picture was of the woman with a girl. The girl had her arms thrown around the woman's frail waist and they both smiled into the camera, though the smile only reached the woman's mouth. Not her eyes. Her eyes were sick. Almost haunted. Lauren couldn't stand to look at the bald despair so she moved her eyes to the face of the girl. A young Lizzie.

So this lady is Lizzie's mother, Lauren glanced back at the frail woman. *She was the one with the perfect life that had turned out to not be so perfect. And Lizzie watched her get sicker and sicker and finally die. That's so sad!* She stared into the eyes of the girl in the picture. There was a fierce, desperate hope in them.

Lauren looked at the rest of the pictures spread out on the book. Lizzie's mother was in every one, but she was no longer vibrant or young. Lauren could almost track the progress of the woman's illness as she looked at each picture in turn. In some she looked not too bad, but the pictures at the bottom of the pile showed her becoming paler and weaker. Sometimes the girl was with her and sometimes her husband, but most of the time she was alone, trying to smile, growing thinner and sicker looking as the pictures progressed.

When the sunlight streaming into the open window hit the first of the photos, Lauren looked up in shock. It was already late afternoon. And she hadn't found anything that would help her understand what was going to happen to the animals.

With her clumsy fingers, Lauren somehow managed to get the photos back into the envelope and the photo album back in the drawer. Then she crept back down the stairs. Lizzie's dad was still in the kitchen. When she entered, he was standing at the counter, pouring himself a cup of coffee. She glanced around the kitchen and noticed the paper and pen on the kitchen table. Silently, she inched forward.

Dear Elizabeth, Lauren read. *I know you don't understand why I sent you away to school. I hope...*

Lauren jumped back as Lizzie's dad walked back to the table, but when he sat down and continued to write she crept forward again. She was surprised when she looked

119

closely at his face. His skin had a gray tinge and his eyes were flat and dull. A tiny shred of pity swelled inside of her, but she squashed it down again.

He's the mean guy who sent Lizzie away, she reminded herself. She looked down at the letter and slowly read the words upside down as he was writing them.

...this letter will explain in a way you can understand. You are the center of my whole world. I would have kept you here at the farm forever if I could have, but I knew that would be selfish. I have to set you up in a new life.

You will not read this letter unless my condition becomes terminal. That means unless it kills me. I have a serious heart disease that the doctors are unable to fix. They say I can go at any time. Of course, I can't tell you this while I'm still alive. More than anything, I don't want you to worry. And that is why I sent you away. I cannot bear to have you see both your parents die. With your mother it was hard enough.

My last request is that you won't hate me for sending you away. It has broken my heart to make you leave. Please never doubt that I love you with everything I am.

I hope you will always understand how thankful I am that you are my daughter. You have been the joy of my life, you and your mother. When I go to meet her, I hope you will carry on, knowing how much we both love you and admire you. I pray you will have a long and beautiful life, Elizabeth, full of love and joy.

Love, Dad.

Chapter Eighteen

Lauren pulled back when she read the last word and watched as Lizzie's dad folded the paper and put it in an envelope. He wrote a few words on the cover of the envelope, but she didn't bother reading them. Her mind was in turmoil. She watched him closely as he stuffed the envelope in his shirt pocket and climbed slowly to his feet. He moved like an old man as he walked to the door and opened it. The dog came to greet him and together they walked toward the barn.

Lauren stood on the porch and watched him shuffle away from her. *He is sick,* she realized. She followed him to the barn and watched as he moved slowly from one empty stall to the next. He laid out the food and water for the animals in their stalls and enclosures, then he moved to the chicken coop and fed the chickens. He came out of the coop a few minutes later, with two eggs in one of his big hands.

"I guess I'll have to start checking twice a day," he said to Jessie and bent to pet the dog on the head. Suddenly, he collapsed to the barn floor and clutched at his chest. The eggs splatted beside him and the dog stepped forward to lick up the fresh yolks. Lizzie's dad's face turned from gray to white as he gasped and fumbled in his pocket. He pulled out a bottle of pills and tried to shake one into his hand, but his movements were too jerky. The pills scattered across the floor. His hands shook as he picked one up and moved it to his mouth. Then he lay still beside the broken eggs.

The effect of the pill was almost immediate. Lauren watched with relief as the color returned to his face. Trooper nickered to him from his stall and Lizzie's dad looked up. "Don't worry, Ben," he said. "I'll be okay this time."

After a time he climbed to his feet. Slowly, he picked up the cleanest pills, brushed them off, and put them back into the pill bottle. Then he limped out the barn door. First he brought in the cows, one by one. Their udders swung heavily beneath them, ready to be milked. He opened the gate to the large pen and laid out some food. Then he left the barn. Within a few minutes, the herd of goats rushed into the barn. The young kids were bouncing around and butting each other. The nanny goats ignored them as they moved toward their dinner. Lauren felt sad as the kids frolicked around her and finally jumped toward their supper, waiting in the pen.

They have no idea of what's going to happen to them, she thought. She watched Lizzie's dad as he shuffled into the barn, far behind them. Slowly he reached for the door. He spoke a few kind words to the goats inside, then pushed the door shut and barred it.

He's so nice to them. You can tell he really cares about his animals. I'm sure he would never leave them here to die unless he couldn't help it.

The man walked back into the deepening twilight. A few minutes later he came back with a big Shire draft horse.

123

"There you go, Lightning," he said as the big horse walked into his stall and buried his nose in his grain. "I know I'm a bit slow tonight. No hard feelings, eh?" Lightning didn't even look up.

"Now just your food and water, Ben," said Lizzie's dad as he walked toward Trooper's stall. The gelding neighed to him as he lifted the empty water bucket from the stall. "I know," Lizzie's dad said. "I miss her too." Lauren watched as he blinked back tears. He patted Trooper on the neck and walked outside to the water trough to fill the bucket.

Suddenly, Lauren heard a crashing noise come from outside. It sounded as if something had fallen against the side of the barn. With her heart in her throat, she rushed outside and around the corner to the water trough. Lizzie's dad was lying on the ground. The water from the bucket soaked the ground all around him.

"Are you okay?" she said as she ran forward, forgetting that he couldn't hear her. She gasped when she saw his face in the evening light. It was so rigid, as if he were using every muscle to not cry out in pain. "Are you okay?" she asked again and reached out to touch him.

"Elizabeth?" he said and Lauren's hand stopped in midair. "How did you get here?"

"You can hear me," she whispered.

"Lizzie, take this letter," he gasped. "I have to make you understand." He reached for the letter that had been in his pocket but it was no longer there. His hand went to the other pocket and then searched the ground for it, then suddenly, he clutched at his chest again.

"Can I help?" begged Lauren. "Please tell me what to do."

"My pills," he gasped.

Lauren reached into his shirt pocket and found the bottle of pills. She tried to wrench the lid off, but her hands seemed even more useless than ever. She couldn't seem to grip the lid of the bottle.

I'm still a ghost, thought Lauren. *So how come he can see and hear me now?* Then she understood the truth. *He's dying,* she realized. The lid came loose in her hand and fell to the ground. *That's why he can see me, because he's close to death. But he thinks I'm his daughter.* She dumped the pills onto her hand and offered them to him. But he didn't take them.

"Too late," he muttered so quietly she almost couldn't hear him. "Forgive me?"

For a moment, Lauren was silent, but then she spoke. "There's nothing to forgive, Daddy," she said. "I love you. I will always love you."

A faint smile swept across his face. "Love you, Lizzie. You're my whole world." He reached out with one weak hand and laid it on top of hers. "Be happy," he said, then just like that, he was gone. Lauren watched as the life drained out of his eyes. His body seemed to become smaller and thinner beneath his clothes.

Lauren jerked her hand away and waited, blinking back tears. No ghost appeared.

He must've gone to where people are supposed to go when they die, she realized. *Not like me.* As the sun disappeared behind the mountain, she stumbled to the barn and fumbled with one of the saddle blankets there. Her fingers couldn't hold it, so finally she draped it over her arm. She carried it back to his body and pulled it over him, then leaned on the side of the barn and covered her face with her hands. She felt weak all of a sudden. Dizzy.

So this is how the animals are abandoned. Lizzie's dad

dies. And no one comes because no one knows he's dead. No one but me. She raised her head, fighting the dizziness with every bit of strength she had.

I'm the only one who can help them. And now's the time to do it.

Chapter Nineteen

She passed a hand over her eyes. Everything was growing darker. She looked at the horizon. The sunset blazed in the west, but she could tell something wasn't normal. It should be brighter, more vibrant.

"What's happening?" she whispered and waved her gray hand in front of her face. Her heart skipped a beat when she noticed how washed out she looked. Not the strong black, gray, and white of that morning and afternoon. She was fading away.

Another wave of dizziness washed over her and she felt the ground move beneath her feet. *This is the worse timing ever. I need to save the animals. Right now, before it's too late!*

Lauren staggered along the edge of the barn and around to the door. It was even darker inside. She fumbled in the shadows along the wall, hoping to find a light switch, but after a moment she gave up and started toward Trooper's stall.

The cows began to moo and shuffle their hooves in the straw when they saw her. They wanted to be milked. Lauren stumbled to the closest stall. She leaned on the door for a moment, then tried to undo the latch. It was even harder to open than the pill bottle. There was a roaring noise in her ears. In horror, Lauren looked down. She was fading fast now. She could hardly see herself in the shadows of the barn, even when she held her hand in front of her eyes.

"I don't have much time Trooper," she said to the gelding as she ran toward his stall. "You're going to have to help me." She leaned against his face and stroked his neck with numb fingers. Trooper leaned down and lipped at the latch on his stall.

"That's right, Trooper," said Lauren in a thin voice. "That's what you do." She reached out and with phantom-like fingers pushed back the latch on his stall. The door swung open.

"Come on," she said and holding his forelock, she led him to the next stall. She could feel the darkness trickling into her consciousness, slowly rising higher and higher. With rubbery, slippery fingers she slid the latch. Trooper stood looking over her shoulder.

The cow in the stall trotted out of the barn as soon as her door swung open and the rest of the cows started to pace in their stalls. They were frightened. Lauren wasn't sure if they were scared of her or nervous because of the change in their routine, but she couldn't waste any time thinking about it. Trooper helped her with the next door, and they had just begun to move to another stall when Lauren remembered. The chickens were at the far end of the barn and she and Trooper were moving away from them.

"I'll be right back," she whispered to Trooper and stumbled toward the end of the barn. The darkness was coming fast now. She felt the bar against the door and pushed it up as hard as she could. The door swung open and Lauren stopped to rest against the doorjamb.

"Just a few more," she told herself as she breathed heavily. "Just a few more stalls."

She felt something touch her back and turned. Trooper stood behind her. Twisting her clumsy fingers in his mane she leaned on his shoulder as she staggered to the remaining stalls. Lauren reached for the next latch but Trooper was there ahead of her with eager lips. Gratefully she leaned on him as the cow galloped out of the barn, her tail in the air and her udders swinging beneath her. Together, Lauren and the horse moved to the next stall.

Finally all the cows were free. Lauren crept toward Lightning's stall, her fingers entwined in Trooper's mane. She had just reached out to undo the latch when Lightning lunged toward Trooper. Trooper jumped away, narrowly missing the snap of Lightning's teeth and Lauren sprawled across the floor.

Oh no. Lightning thinks that Trooper's after his oats, thought Lauren. *How am I going to undo his stall without Trooper's help?* She took a deep breath and pushed herself up with her arms. She staggered toward the stall door and somehow found the latch. But her fingers wouldn't work. Lauren fought for a grip, but her hands hardly existed anymore. When the pale outline of her fingers looked like they were in the right position, Lauren jerked the latch back. And it moved a tiny bit. No more.

Lauren focused all her strength on the terrible truth. *Lightning is going to die if I can't undo this latch. He'll be locked up in this barn without any more food or water. No one is going to come here for a long time. No one knows that Lizzie's dad is dead and he won't be discovered until it's too late.*

"Trooper, help," Lauren called to the young horse, but the thudding in her ears was growing so loud that she didn't know if Trooper had even heard her. She held onto the wall as she staggered into the empty stall next to Lightning's. At the rear of the stall, she reached through the bars toward his oat bucket and fumbled for his halter. Finally her fingers wrapped around the cheek strap. Her grip was too weak to hold him, but Lightning didn't know that and stood obediently.

"Now, Trooper," she whispered, her strength almost gone. The halter jerked out of her hands. Lauren looked up in time to see Lightning chase Trooper from the barn. As the two dark shapes faded into the evening, a great sense of relief washed over her. Lightning was free. They were all free.

I can let go now, Lauren thought. *I don't have to fight it anymore.*

Then she heard them in their pen. The goats. She had forgotten about the goats. The darkness was almost over-powering her and the thud in her head was so loud that Lauren wondered how she had heard them. With all her strength gone, Lauren crumpled to the floor of the barn.

Trooper will save them, won't he? she reasoned. *He knows how to undo the latches now.* Then a feeling of dread washed over her. *But the goat's door has a bar, just like the chicken coop. And Trooper doesn't know how to open a barred door, only latched doors.*

With strength she didn't know she had, Lauren crawled out of the empty stall toward the goats' pen. Everything was dark now and her heartbeat boomed like thunder in her ears. A hundred times she wanted to lie down and give up. *I can't let them die,* she told herself, over and over. *I can't let them die.*

After forever, she felt the wood of the goat's door be-neath her hands. She slid her hands upward against the wood, not caring about the slivers and splinters that stabbed into her ghostly palms. There was no pain to feel. When her hands stopped against a solid form, she knew she had found the bar across the door. She pushed up with all of her remaining strength. The bar slid upward in its bracket. But not far enough.

"Trooper, help me," whispered Lauren. She didn't think the gelding was close enough to hear her, but she couldn't call any louder. She had nothing left to give. She collapsed on the floor beside the door.

I've failed, she realized. *They're going to die because I'm not strong enough.*

Then she felt him walk toward her, his hooves vibrating the barn floor with each step. "Trooper, lift it up," she whispered. "Watch me and lift it the rest of the way up."

Lauren blindly rose to her knees and felt along the wood above her head until the bar was again in her hands. She was able to push once more, weakly, ineffectively. And then she spiralled into darkness.

The last thing she heard was Trooper's neigh. It fell with her down a long dark tunnel, echoed around and against her, pushing and buffeting her, on and on and on into forever.

Chapter Twenty

The neigh came again and again. Lauren struggled to wake, but her eyes didn't want to open. "Trooper," she whispered and tried to move. Pain shot through her body and Lauren gasped.

The neigh came again, even more insistent. "Trooper," Lauren called and opened her eyes to stare at the barn ceiling, at morning sunlight streaming through cracks between the boards, at the broken ladder lying on top of her.

"Trooper, I'm here!" She could hear Trooper's neigh come from outside. He sounded so close. "Did you untie yourself, Trooper? You did, didn't you? You're my hero, Troops!" She shoved the broken boards off and struggled to sit up. Her back and arm burned as she pushed herself to a sitting position. Her upper arm was covered with dried blood. A raw, red gash lay beneath the rust-colored flakes.

Tiger jumped onto her leg, making her wince. "But who cares if it hurts a bit, hey, Tiger? I didn't die! And it'll make a cool scar. How many people can say they've fallen from a barn loft?" she said and stroked the tabby kitten's back. She took a deep breath. "I can't believe it was all just a dream. I thought I was dead. I thought I'd

132

been sent back in time. It all seemed so real!" A deep purr erupted from the kitten's scrawny body.

"Where's Spunky?" Lauren looked around until she saw the orange kitten's tail poking out from behind one of the stall doors. *Lightning's stall*, she thought and then reminded herself it had only been a dream.

"Hey buddy," she said and carefully climbed to her feet. Thankfully, nothing seemed to be broken, but every muscle in her body ached. She bent to pick up Tiger and slowly straightened, the tabby kitten in her arms. Then she looked toward the stall. Spunky's tail was gone.

He must be inside the stall, she thought. The stall door hung askew and a puzzled look crept over Lauren's face. She was sure the door had been closed before. She had looked over it to see if there were bones inside. She caught her breath and looked down the line of stalls. Could it be? *Maybe it wasn't a dream! All the doors are open!*

Eagerly, she approached Lightning's stall and peered inside. Dust covered the disintegrating straw. An orange kitten lay in the center of the space, looking up at her with friendly, playful eyes. But there were no bones. As fast as her stiff body allowed her to move, Lauren hurried down the line of stalls. Not one held the remains of a dead animal, horse or cow. The chicken coop door was open and there was nothing in the coop but more dust, straw and dirt. They had all been freed to find their own food and water until rescue came. And she *had* done it. It wasn't a dream!

And the goats? Lauren turned toward their pen, afraid of what she would see. Then she leaped in the air, instantly forgetting her stiffness. "Yes!" she screamed. "Awesome!" The door to the goats' pen stood open.

133

Tiger leaped from her arms and raced to stand beside Spunky, now washing his paws in front of Lightning's stall. "Sorry, Tiger," said Lauren. "I didn't mean to scare you. It's just that it wasn't a dream! That means that none of the animals died! Trooper and I saved them, years and years ago. Long before you were born." A wave of euphoria swept over Lauren and she spun in a circle on the dusty floor, her arms wide. The kittens looked at her as if she had gone mad. She stopped when she heard Trooper neigh again.

"Troops," she yelled as she ran toward the door. Her muscles were becoming more limber with use, though she still felt sore in places where she was sure dark bruises were blooming on her skin. "We did it! We freed them!" She reached the double doors and peered through the crack between them.

Trooper was a short distance from the door looking back at Lauren with bright inquisitive eyes. "Hey, buddy. You'll have to go for help," said Lauren. "I can't open the door and there's no other way out. There's even wire over the chicken coop windows."

Trooper neighed and tossed his head. The lead rope pulled taut against his halter. "Is your rope tangled up, boy?" she asked. Her heart sank as her eyes focused behind Trooper. One side of the porch on the old house had collapsed, and the corner beam Trooper had been tied to was gone. To free himself, he had pulled back and jerked the rotting wood from its foundation. Then apparently he had dragged the pillar behind him to the barn.

"Oh no," the soft words escaped from her lips. Trooper might have had the strength to drag the pillar to the barn door, but he couldn't pull it all the way home. It would get caught up somewhere. In fact, it was a miracle he had

134

made it this far, there were so much brushy vegetation. And if Trooper couldn't go for help, how would she get out of the barn?

Trooper pulled tight against his halter rope again scooting the pillar a few more inches toward her.

"Troops, don't. You're going to hurt yourself. You're going to rub sores on your nose."

Trooper stepped forward and tugged again. Lauren could see the bushes shaking behind him as the pillar scooted a little closer. He was only half a body length away now. "Stop, Trooper. Stop. You're hurting yourself." Lauren begged. She could see the raw redness under the noseband of his halter now. The nylon was cutting right into his flesh. She banged on the door, hoping that the sound would scare him back, but when she peeked through the crack again, he had only scooted the pillar closer. He reached his head toward the door, and when he couldn't quite touch it, he jerked on the rope again. The pillar slid closer.

"Trooper, your poor nose," said Lauren. She tried to poke her fingers through the crack between the two doors but it was too narrow. Trooper sniffed at her fingers. Then, when he moved his head away, he bumped the bar with his muzzle. At first Lauren thought it was an accident. Only when Trooper reached out and bumped it again, making the bar slide up an inch in its bracket, did she understand.

That's the answer! she realized in an instant. *I showed him how to unbar the goat's door years and years ago. And now he knows how to open barred doors too, not just the latched ones!*

"Trooper, you remember the goats!" she called, her voice tense with excitement. "You remember how you

135

opened their door. You are so amazing!" Trooper sniffed at the board, then put his nose under it and pushed again. It slid up in the bracket another inch, then fell back down to the bottom.

With a great effort, Lauren controlled her enthusiasm. "Good boy," she repeated and pushed the doors outward. She had to keep a steady pressure against the board so it wouldn't slide back down, but not push so hard that Trooper couldn't move it up. When he bumped it again and it slid upward, Lauren was able to keep it in place.

"Do it again, Troops," she said, her heart racing. Just two or three more bumps and she would be free. He pushed again and Lauren saw the dark form of the board slide up another inch against the brightness of the crack.

"One more time, Trooper," she called from her side of the door. Trooper nickered in response and when he bumped the door, Lauren pushed against it. The door swung open, almost hitting Trooper in the face. He jumped back and Lauren staggered out into the morning light. Laughing, she flung her arms around the gelding's neck.

"You are the most amazing horse in the entire world, Trooper," she gushed into his mane. Then she pulled back and kissed his sore nose. "The most wonderful, smartest, most beautiful horse that ever existed!"

A tiny mew came from behind her and Lauren turned to find Spunky and Tiger blinking in the bright sunlight. She scooped them into her arms and snuggled them close. Rumbling purrs vibrated their tiny bodies.

"Trooper saved us," whispered Lauren, and was tempted to spin in a circle again. Just in time, she remembered how she had scared Tiger the last time and stopped herself. "Now I'm going to introduce you to him. Our hero. Don't be scared because he's huge. He's just a big softie."

136

Suddenly, Lauren's mouth fell open. She snapped it shut when Tiger put his paw on her tongue. Slowly, she turned toward the golden gelding.

"Trooper, I almost left the goats," she whispered. Her knees felt weak. "I almost didn't have enough strength. If I had collapsed just ten seconds sooner, you couldn't have saved me. You wouldn't have known how."

It was so close, she thought. *What if I had listened to my own doubts, or decided that I'd saved enough animals and left them? What if I'd been pushed back into my own time just one minute sooner?*

Lauren looked up at Trooper. "You saved me, Trooper. But in a way I helped you save me." She glanced down at the kittens. "So I'm the hero too, guys," she added and smiled. "You don't look too impressed, but just wait until I tell you all about it. Later, when we're back at Aunt April and Uncle Chris's. They probably have the whole police force out looking for us. And Dad's probably here too." Lauren's face dropped. *And that means my mom will be here.*

Trooper nuzzled her shoulder. "I'm not mad at you, Troops. I could never be mad at you. It's just my mom." She paused and looked down at the kittens nestled in her arms. "I don't know what I'm going to say to her. I still can't believe she just left Dad and me. And that everyone lied about her being dead."

Lauren leaned against Trooper's shoulder and snuggled the kittens closer. When she spoke again, her voice was rough with emotion. "And I can never accept her back. Not after she abandoned us, Trooper. She didn't want me before, and now it's too late. As far as I'm concerned, she really *is* dead."

138

Chapter Twenty-One

Within a few minutes, Lauren had the kittens inside Lightning's old feedbag. They settled on top of the rags she put at the bottom and closed their eyes, their bellies still round from their feast the night before. She set the feedbag on the ground to untie Trooper from the pillar and adjusted his halter so it wasn't rubbing the sore spot on his nose, then picked up the feedbag and led Trooper toward the old road. They only went a few steps before Trooper stopped.

"What's wrong, Troops?" she asked. Trooper tossed his head and took a step backwards. Lauren walked back to his head. She wasn't about to doubt him now, not after he freed her and the kittens. Trooper nickered quietly and turned to walk back to the barn.

Lauren pulled on the rope when he tried to step inside. "Whoa, Trooper. Wait until I block the door open." She rolled a stone in front of the open door, then followed him into the barn.

The gelding stopped where Lizzie's dad had first fallen. He sniffed the ground as Lauren patted his shoulder. "What are you doing, buddy?" she asked. "Why did you want to come in here again?"

Trooper touched the farm machinery parked against the wall with his nose, then pawed the floor. He looked back at Lauren and neighed.

"What's wrong, Trooper?" she asked again, her eyes puzzled. "I don't understand."

The gelding struck out again with his hoof and the clang of his shoe against the rusted metal echoed through the barn. Lauren stroked his side. "You're trying to show me something," she whispered in sudden awe. She bent down and looked beneath the machine. A dusty envelope laid there – a letter, the one Lizzie's dad had written.

It must've slipped from his pocket when he collapsed after leaving the chicken coop, realized Lauren. *Then maybe the dog accidentally pushed it under the machine when he was licking up the eggs.*

Lauren reached to pick it up. "And you saw it fall, Trooper," she said, straightening and looking into his eyes. "You were in the barn and you saw it slide under the machine. And all these years later, you still remember." Trooper looked back at her with dark eyes. Lauren shook her head. She didn't understand. How could Trooper know the letter was important? But somehow he did.

"You're one in a million, Troops." Lauren looked down at the letter in her hand. "So she never got to read it. Poor Lizzie. I wonder if Aunt April knows who she is and where she is now? Lizzie should know her dad didn't send her away because he didn't love her. He was just trying to take care of her."

Lauren took a tentative step toward the door. When Trooper followed her, she led him out of the barn and toward the overgrown road. Halfway there, she walked him to one of the old fences, climbed up the wooden rails and slid onto his back, being careful not to jostle the kittens.

140

At the fallen gate, she pulled the gelding to a stop. Together they looked back.

Lauren smiled. "It doesn't look scary anymore, does it, Troops? The animals are at peace. They went on to lives with other people and none of them died here." She smiled again as she thought of the frisky little goats, the productive chickens, the pretty jersey cows. Lightning, big, strong, steady Lightning, afraid that Trooper was going to steal his oats and almost dying for his greediness.

"And the dog, Jessie, would have been adopted too. Every one of the animals. Except for the cats." She looked down at the kittens, still asleep in Lightning's feedbag. "Your ancestors probably went wild before Lizzie's dad was discovered. But now it's really over, kitties. The final orphans are being adopted. You." She sighed and took one last, long look at the house, at the barn, at the overgrown yard and fields beyond. *It was such a pretty place here once,* she thought before turning away. *I'll never forget it.*

Trooper's hoofbeats on the overgrown road were muffled and rhythmic. Slowly they wound their way through the brush. It took them half an hour to reach the spot where she'd had her battle with Trooper, where he had tried to take her to the old homestead when Lauren wanted him to go back to Aunt April's. *That was only yesterday,* she reminded herself. *It seems so long ago. So much has happened since then.*

Trooper's head shot into the air and his ears strained forward. Instinctively, Lauren pulled back on the lead rope. Then she heard it. Crackling branches. Someone or something was coming along the old overgrown road. Lauren's heart lurched when she caught movement in the vegetation. Then she saw a flash of blue cloth. A breath of relief exploded from her lungs.

"Don't worry, Troops. Its just people. They might even be searching for us." She paused and listened to them come closer. "Hello!" she called.

"Lauren! Lauren, is that you!" Her dad's voice, full of strain and relief. And barking. Sweetie's barking.

"Dad! Sweetie! It's me! And Trooper!"

She slid from Trooper's back and pulled him toward the crackling as fast as she could go, the kitten's bag thumping against her leg. She heard a questioning mew come from the feedbag. "It's okay, guys," she had time to gasp and then Sweetie leaped out of the bushes. She planted her feet on Lauren's chest, trying to reach her face to lick her, between joyous whines.

In a split second, the kittens were out of the feedbag and halfway up a tree. Lauren dropped to her knees and hugged Sweetie, then called to the kittens. "It's okay, Tiger. Spunky. Its just Sweetie. And Dad. You'll like them. I promise."

Then her dad was in front of her. Lauren jumped to her feet and his arms were around her. He spun her around and seemed to be laughing and crying all at the same time.

"It's okay, Dad!" yelled Lauren. "I'm okay. Really, I'm okay. And just wait until I tell you what happened. I found..."

Her voice stopped short when a blond woman stepped out from the bushes behind them. Lauren stiffened in her father's arms and he lowered her to the ground.

"Mom," said Lauren. The word held no warmth. No welcome. No forgiveness. She felt nauseous.

Sweetie and Lauren's dad were silent, their eyes on

Lauren. The woman froze as if Lauren's voice had struck her.

Only Trooper stepped forward with a low whinny of greeting, deep in his throat.

Chapter Twenty-Two

"Lauren, let me explain," the woman said, tears catching at her voice.

"What's there to explain?" said Lauren, as hard as ice. "Why you abandoned us? Why you ran out on your daughter and your husband? Why you're a horrible person?"

"Just listen to her, Lauren," said her dad. "There's something you don't know."

Lauren looked up at him, speechless for a moment. "You may have forgiven her, but I can't. I won't! Ever! She doesn't deserve us, Dad. She ran out on us."

"Yes, but…" Lauren's mom stopped speaking. Tears streamed down her cheeks. "She's right," she added in a choked voice. "I shouldn't have come back. I shouldn't have…" She turned and staggered away from them. Lauren's dad was at her side in an instant. He put his arm around her and turned her back toward Lauren.

"Lauren, it's your choice whether to accept your mom back or not," he said. His face was weary. "We will *both* abide by your decision. The only thing I ask is that you listen to why she went away."

"But Dad…" Lauren couldn't believe it. He was taking *her* side.

"No buts. Will you listen or not?"

Lauren's jaw tightened and she looked at the ground. She kicked at the pine needles. "I'll listen," she finally muttered. "But it won't make any difference."

Lauren's mom dried her eyes on the sleeve of her sweatshirt and took a deep breath. When she spoke her voice was shaky and weak. "I didn't leave because I didn't love you, Lauren. I left because I did. I was in a car accident. That much you know. It wasn't a serious accident. I was only in the hospital for minor injuries and observation. But when I was there, the doctors discovered I had cancer. After they did some tests, they told me I had six months to live. A year at the most. And I couldn't bear to have you see me die. I didn't know what to do. Then, the night before I was to be released from the hospital, the answer came to me. I would run away and then the people I loved wouldn't have to watch me die."

She paused and Lauren's dad pulled her closer.

"So you *knew* she was still alive, Dad?"

"I knew, Lauren," admitted her dad. "She left a note for me with one of the nurses. But I didn't know where she'd gone. I looked everywhere. I even hired a detective. But she just disappeared. And…" He looked down at his wife. "And – I'm sorry, honey – after a year, I stopped looking. By then I thought it was too late. That the cancer would have taken you from us anyway."

"But it didn't!" Lauren was almost yelling now. "Why didn't you come back after six months? Or even a year? Why did you wait so long?"

"It took me years to get better. After six months, I was so sick, and after a year, I wished I were dead. Without you, without your dad, my life meant nothing to me. But I *didn't* die. And then I started to get better. Slowly. At

145

first I didn't believe it was really happening. I thought I was imagining it. But then I knew I wasn't. Just this last spring, the tests came up completely negative. The cancer was cured."

"And you thought we'd accept you back?" asked Lauren.

"No, I didn't. It's more like I couldn't stay away. I don't blame you if you never forgive me, if you never accept me back."

"So, you know what you did was wrong?" Lauren's voice was harsh and bitter.

Her mom didn't answer right away and Lauren spoke again. "You're not sure, are you?"

Slowly, the older woman shook her head. "I don't know what I'd do if I had to do it over. It's hard watching someone die. You don't know how hard."

"I do know."

"What?" Both Lauren's parent's spoke together.

"I watched a man die *yesterday*. And he did what you did. He separated himself from his daughter. He died begging for her forgiveness, begging for her to understand."

"What are you talking about, Lauren?" asked her dad, stepping forward and kneeling in front of her.

She looked down into his worried eyes. "It's true, Dad. And I saw more," she said, her voice softening. She looked at her mom. "I saw photos of his wife and their daughter and the woman was dying. But *she* didn't send her daughter away. You could see her fading away in the pictures and you could see how much she hated to die. But until she had to leave, she refused to go. She didn't *abandon* her family. She stayed with them as long as she could. She knew they were meant to be together. And that's all that mattered to her."

Lauren watched her mom's face grow pale. "Where did you see these pictures?"

"What does it matter to you?"

"It matters." Her mom's voice was soft.

"In an old farmhouse at the end of this road."

Lauren's dad was on his feet in a second but he wasn't quick enough. Lauren's mom clutched at Trooper's mane as she sank to the ground.

"Beth. Beth." He lifted her head into his lap and patted her cheek. Trooper nuzzled her shoulder. Sweetie licked the tears from her face.

"Is she okay, Dad?" asked Lauren, worried now. "What happened?"

"She fainted. She'll be okay. She does that sometimes when she gets super stressed," he said.

"She's stressed because of me?"

"Yes. And because of what you just said. About the farmhouse."

Lauren's mom opened her eyes. She breathed deeply for a few seconds, then weakly pushed herself to a sitting position.

"What's going on? Mom? Dad?" Lauren could tell there was more they hadn't told her.

"The daughter, the girl in the pictures," said Lauren's mom. "She was me. My mom, your grandmother, died when I was ten years old. That was the pain I wanted to spare you. The pain of watching your mother die."

Chapter Twenty-Three

Lauren stepped back, stunned. That girl, Lizzie. That was her mom. Of course. Lizzie, Beth: they were both from the name Elizabeth. So the girl in the barn, the one she had comforted, was her own mother. And the man who died in front of her, the man she had forgiven for Lizzie, was her grandfather. Her voice was quiet when she finally spoke. "Mom, are you still angry at…Grandpa for sending you away?"

"How did you know I was angry?"

"Are you?" Lauren's voice was firmer. This was the time for her mom to answer questions, not her.

"Yes," her mom whispered and looked at the ground.

Lauren pulled the letter from her pocket and knelt beside her mom. "Read this."

Beth opened the crumbling old envelope and gingerly removed the letter. As she read, her eyes filled with tears.

"He did what you did," Lauren said bitterly. "He broke up his family. By trying to save you pain, he caused you more. At least you knew your mom loved you and didn't want to get rid of you." She paused when her mother's face went pale again. "You were wrong to leave," she concluded firmly.

It was a full minute before Beth spoke and when she

did, her voice cracked with emotion. "Oh, Lauren, how could I have been so wrong? Alan, Lauren, I'm sorry. I know that sounds lame. I know it's not nearly enough. How can I ask you to forgive me when I abandoned you? How can I ask you to welcome me…" She stopped, no longer able to continue. Her eyes pleaded with Lauren, speaking louder than words ever could.

Lauren didn't know what to say. How could she tell her mom to go away? But how could she just accept her back as if nothing had happened? *Maybe she meant well, but it cost me and Dad so much pain, so much heartache! But then, she was doing what she thought was right.*

As Lauren stared at her mother, the blond hair seemed to lighten. The lines on her face smoothed. She became Lizzie again. And once more, in her mind's eye, Lauren saw Lizzie crumpled at Trooper's hooves, sobbing. She saw her trying to act strong as she climbed into the car, being driven away, broken-hearted and feeling rejected.

The animals aren't the only ones I have the power to rescue, Lauren suddenly realized. *I can save my family too. I'm the only one who can.*

"I forgive you, Mom." The words were barely a whisper at first. Then Lauren spoke them louder, "I forgive you. You shouldn't have left. You should have given us the chance to take care of you." She felt tears come to her eyes and didn't even try to stop them. "You should have stayed with us, even if you were sick. Like Grandma did. We were a family. *Are* a family. Right?"

"Right, Kiddo" whispered her Mom. "I'm going to do everything I can to make it up to you. I promise."

Lauren couldn't help but smile through her tears. Maybe that crazy nickname had originated with her mom and not her dad.

Lauren's dad held his hand out and helped his wife to her feet, then he circled his arms around both of them, pulling them into a hug. For a moment, it felt strange to Lauren to feel her mother's body right next to hers. Then her mom's arm went around her and it was almost as if she had never left.

When the hug finally loosened, Lauren looked up into her dad's serious eyes. "Now young lady, you have a lot to answer to. Running off like that and scaring everyone half to death."

"But I didn't mean to, Dad," said Lauren. "I was trapped in that old barn. The door blew shut in the storm. And then Trooper got me out, or really, in a way, I got myself out. Or we did it together. You see there were all these animals that died there…" She paused, not knowing how to start.

"The animals didn't die," said Lauren's mom, her voice puzzled. "They were all found wandering around the property. The estate lawyers found good homes for every one of them."

"But they *did* die, until…well, I'll tell you in a minute. It's a long story," said Lauren. "First, I was wondering, do you still own that old farm, Mom?" It seemed strange to say the word "Mom" again.

"Yes, I never could sell it. I loved it too much as a child. And my parents loved it too."

"So why did you let it go to ruin?" asked Lauren.

"There were so many heartaches there. My mother dying. My dad sending me away. All those years I thought he didn't love me, that maybe he even despised me. And then there was… no, its silly."

"What?" Lauren and her dad asked together.

"You'll think I'm dumb."

151

"No, we won't," said Lauren.

"Well, there was all the stuff that happened with my parents, but I also lost my best friend. My *only* friend really, after my mother died."

"No, don't say anymore," interrupted Lauren. She took her mom's hand in hers and led her back to Trooper. Beth stroked the gelding's nose. "Don't you recognize him?" Lauren asked.

Beth raised her hand to the crescent shaped star. "He looks just like… but it can't be. The lawyers sold him with the other animals before I could stop them. And besides, he couldn't still be alive, could he?" Hope was starting to quicken her voice. "That was twenty years ago. Or more. How can it be my Ben?"

Trooper lowered his head and nickered to her.

"But it *is* him, Mom. It's your Ben and my Trooper. One of his other owners must have changed his name."

"But how can it be?" Tears caught at her voice again. She turned to Lauren. "How did you know it was him?"

"Like I said," Lauren answered, raising her eyebrows. "It's a long story." A mewing noise interrupted her. "Just a minute, guys," she called. "I'll get you down in a second."

Her dad turned toward the kittens. "Who do they belong to?" he asked.

"Me. I mean us. I guess I have to explain that too," said Lauren. She twisted her fingers in Trooper's mane. "We can keep them, can't we, Dad?"

"Of course. This is the day for increasing the size of our family, isn't it?" He grinned. "Now let's get back to this long story you mentioned."

"Are you sure you're ready? For the whole thing?"

When her parents nodded, Lauren began.

152